HOLMES & ADLER

After the Falls

A Death at the Derby

Bernard J Samuelson

Dedicated to my one true love, Fran, and soul mate for all these years

AFTER THE FALLS

Preface

Times of London Obituaries May 7, 1891

Sherlock Holmes of 221B Baker Street perished on May 4, 1891, at Reichenbach Falls in Switzerland, Mr. Holmes was 37 years old, and a ...

INDIA

October 7, 1892

The grueling events of the last year and a half spread over two continents have ended.

CHAPTER 1

Arrival in the United States
October 28, 1892

T hree weeks later, it is a calm sunny day as the S.S Juanita docks at the Port of New York from Valencia.

Reginald Wallace, an Englishman, and resident of London, is on vacation to the United States; he passes through customs; secures his luggage, and goes to his hotel near the railroad station connecting New York City to nearby New Jersey.

Long-Awaited Journey
October 29, 1892

T he following morning, Wallace leaves his hotel for the railway to New Jersey.

He is restless and nervous about the task he is about to perform. Never having been in this situation except in his imagination.

He arrives at his destination at one in the afternoon. He checks his luggage at the station, hails a carriage, and starts on the most exciting ride of his life.

The same morning, she arises early dresses for riding, has breakfast and when finished finds a stable boy with her mare, Sally, ready for a nice run and leisurely ride around her estate. First, she rides to the practice track for a brisk gallop with Sally.

Exhilarated by the morning ride she inspects the stables, and finds everything in fine order, as always. After a goodbye to Sally, she turns her over to a stable lad for grooming.

She walks back to the house. Now she must bathe; get dressed for the day, and it should be a relaxing day with nothing planned.

He is deep in thought during the carriage ride from the railway station to her house. The weather is cloudy and mildly warm. Turning off the main road, the carriage carries him down a tree-lined carriageway, and the trees have changed to their Fall colors. The carriage pulls up in front of a modern Victorian house. He exits the carriage asking the driver to wait telling him, "I may not be very long, but if it seems I shall be longer, I will ask a servant to pay you." The cabbie nods his assent.

He hesitates, gathers himself, walks up the stairs across the porch and pulls the bell cord.

The door is opened and he is greeted by the butler, who asks, "May I help you, sir?"

"Yes, you may. Is the lady of the house in residence?"

"Yes, milady is here. May I inquire about your business?"

"Yes, I would like you to deliver a note to her; I shall await her reply."

The butler says, "Please come in, have a seat in the entrance hall, and I will take your note to milady."

"Thank you."

He watches the butler disappear into the house with his missive. He sits in a somewhat agitated manner. The long entrance hall has stylish paintings of many European scenes, interspersed with various horse paintings, colts with their mothers, and photographs of horses dashing for the finish line.

He hopes that he is not being impertinent by calling upon her at this time. He continues to wait patiently but nervously in the entrance hall.

CHAPTER 3

The Meeting

H is wait is rewarded by the arrival of a maid.

Who says, "Sir, please follow me, my mistress is on the veranda."

He thanks her, and does as directed. After a brief, but swift walk the doors to the veranda are opened by the maid, who announces, "Milady, the gentleman."

The veranda faces a sea of Fall flowers, a well-cared-for lawn, a stable in the distance with a short race track, and a pasture where several mares are awaiting the birth of their young early next year.

Mrs. Irene Adler Norton, as elegant and radiant, as ever, rises from her chair and crosses the veranda to greet him as the maid leaves closing the veranda doors.

She says, "What does this note mean, 'Briony Clergyman? I was at Briony Lodge in London and only met an injured clergyman there, and are you", she pauses; exclaiming, "it is not possible, you are dead, Mr. Sherlock Holmes! Dr. Watson wrote of your demise after you fell into the Reichenbach Falls gorge. You left a note before you engaged Professor Moriarty. How can this be?"

"I am sorry, I shocked you, no, Mrs. Norton, I am not dead although I have changed my appearance with the van dyke and the shading and cut of my hair. As to my death, I will tell you all about later, if I have the chance."

Standing there she says, rather coldly, "Mr. Holmes, this is quite a surprise, has the King another request of me?"

"No, Mrs. Norton, I am not here at the request of the King. I am not using my real name, since I am supposed to be dead, I am using the name, Reginald Wallace."

"Not using your real name; there must be a story there."

"Yes, there is, but it can wait."

"I must apologize for my rude behavior, please have a seat."

She rings a bell; the maid returns and she says; "Mildred please bring us tea, is tea to your liking Mr. Hol..er Wallace?"

"Yes, tea would be most appreciated."

The maid replies, "Yes Milady" and leaves to get the tea.

Mrs. Norton says, " I am at a loss for words since I do not know whatever you could want from me after the ordeal with the crown prince."

He sits rather uncomfortably and looks at her, thinking she is even more beautiful than he remembered, and lost in his thoughts, he almost misses what she said.

Coming back to himself, says, "I am not here as an agent or investigator on anyone's behalf, except my own."

She says curtly, " I do not understand, what is your behalf?"

CHAPTER 4

Tea and History

He becomes reluctant to tell her why he is here. She looks at him quizzically. At that moment the maid returns with the tea and teacakes; sets it upon the tea table, to serve the tea, when Mrs. Norton says, "Thank you, Mildred, I shall serve, please go about your other duties."

"Yes, Milady" and she leaves the veranda closing the doors after her.

Mrs. Norton serves the tea and offers teacakes which Sherlock politely declines. Once served selects a teacake takes a bite, settles back in her seat, sipping her tea, and once again looks quizzically at him waiting to hear his response to her inquiry.

Before he can reply, she intervenes, "I noticed in Dr. Watson's writings, all of which I have read, you had shown no interest in any female, except me in 'A Scandal in Bohemia' and why was that?"

He nervously takes another sip of his tea.

"When the Crown Prince employed me, I was intrigued a woman had held her own against his numerous attempts to retrieve the photograph. I took the case because I was curious and the funds presented, although princely, were to me secondary."

She is becoming agitated and selects a second biscuit, "I find your reason interesting, but where pray tell is this leading us?"

"Please bear with me, I will get there shortly. As we know, you saw through my disguise as the injured clergyman which led to your hasty departure for the continent with your husband taking the photograph with you. I am curious do you still have it?"

"Is this what you are after?"

"No, no, I am just normally curious."

"The photograph took up residence in the channel on our honeymoon trip to the continent."

" A grand way to dispose of it."

Pausing, "Yet, had it never existed, I would not be here. As you know from reading Watson's account of your wedding, you gave me a sovereign which I still carry as my watch fob."

Laughingly, she says, "I had no idea at the time, and only learned it from Dr. Watson's account."

When she had recovered, he goes on, "The day you left and we found you were gone, the Crown Prince was ecstatic. He offered his ring as a reward for a job well done; as you know I declined; he asked what reward I would like, and for a reward, I took your photograph keeping it to this day."

Finally, she speaks, "Mr. Holmes, over the years, I have reminisced about the incident with the Crown Prince, my encounter with you, and wondered what you might be doing. I began to read about your exploits in the Strand, I knew at once the Bohemia story was about me; naming me 'The Woman'".

"Yes, you are 'The Woman'. I instructed Watson to use the term when describing you in the unlikely event you read any of his scribblings."

She was silent and serene.

CHAPTER 5

Feelings

Sherlock sighs, which is not in his nature, and says, "This is difficult for me, in my profession, I have encountered many females who were either a victim or a perpetrator of a crime. None of the former victims were of any interest to me on a personal level, and the perpetrators were far beyond any interest of mine. After all these years, whenever I met a woman I compared her to you with none being worthy of comparison. I have to say I thought of you often always wishing you happiness. When I heard of your husband's death, I had to use all my will power to keep from coming here to comfort you. Such an action would have been unseemly, so I have impatiently waited. Since the falls, I have been a hunted man by a criminal organization bent on killing me. I have eluded them for nearly a year and a half and finally the last of my pursuers has been captured leaving me free to travel to the United States. If I return too soon to England, it may start again. Facing death during the last seventeen months has made me steadfast that I must see you once again, and let you know how I feel."

She remains silent for a time; then says, "I am pleased you escaped from your hunters, but I now understand, I am a task you must complete before these criminals kill you on your return to England and if that be the case. May you elude your pursuers for many more years; now please see yourself out."

Sherlock arises; instead of making his way to exit, moves towards her saying, "Please do not dismiss me so. As those, who know me best see me as a calculating machine without the sensibilities most people have, I have banished those emotions from my persona, save except for you. I believe from the first time I saw you until this day, we were and are soul mates. You are definitely not a task to be completed."

Hesitating he continues, "I am here to express my wish to be with 'The Woman' for as long as she may have me. Once again, you are not a task, but the beginning of what I hope is a life long journey; I wish to have you share with me"

She remains seated and remains silent for several heartbeats, but to Sherlock, it seems an eternity.

She shifts from the chair's edge and indicates he should be re-seated.

"Frankly, at first I was uneasy with the story, but the more I thought about it I became immensely proud to have been awarded that title. As I said, I read all of the stories and I began to see a man of superior intellect with unbelievable insight into the people he encountered, but a lonely unfulfilled person, who found artificial solace in cocaine. I believe if you fill your emptiness with appropriate human affection and companionship, you would truly be even a greater practitioner of your unique avocation."

"I appreciate your candor, and as to my vice, these last seventeen months, I believe have cured me of this affliction, but it is day-to-day. A please permit me to apologize for my rude behavior, my parents tried as they might not persuade me to accept or understand the social graces. I was always more concerned with other disciplines; considered those actions as unnecessary to my avocation; although I admit it was sometimes uncomfortable to be treated like a real human being, and not a man with peculiar skills."

CHAPTER 6

Dinner Invitation

S he is thoughtful for a little while, then asks, "Will you have dinner with me this evening. I am curious about what happened after the falls, and I would like to know what else you have on your mind."

"Yes, I would like it greatly, but I must make arrangements for suitable accommodations for my stay in the vicinity, and gather my meager belongings from the railway station."

She rings the bell, Mildred appears.

"Mildred, please have Clarence come here."

"Yes, milady."

Several minutes later, Clarence, the butler, arrives, "Yes, milady."

"Mr. Wallace needs suitable local accommodations for an extended stay and he needs his luggage from the railway station."

"Yes, milady."

Sherlock interjects, "I need to release the carriage I had from the train station and pay the man. I will go out and pay him."

Mrs. Norton says, "No need, give Mildred the money and she will pay him."

Clarence says, "Milady, I believe the Shelton Arms is a very nice hotel with all the best in facilities; it is, as you know, only three miles from here, has telephone service and carriage rentals."

She looks at Sherlock, "Is it suitable for your needs?"

"Yes, it sounds very good."

Clarence asks, "Now for your luggage, do you have the tags, sir?"

"Yes, I do." He takes them out and puts them into the out-stretched hand of the butler.

Clarence says, "I will have Ronnie go to the railway station; re-trieve Mr. Wallace's luggage and take it to the hotel."

Irene says, "Thank you, one more thing, Clarence. Mr. Wallace will be having dinner here tonight. Have the coachman take Mr. Wallace to the hotel to freshen up before dinner."

Looking at Sherlock she says, "Dinner is at seven, and in America, unlike England, we do not formally dress for dinner. My home is basically a horse farm."

Sherlock says, "Until tonight.", he leaves and meets the coach-man and makes his way to the Shelton Arms, overcome with a feeling of elation, he had not had in many years, if ever.

The Shelton Arms is a very nice hotel with all the necessary amenities. His luggage arrives shortly after he did, he sends a suit and shirt to be pressed, and shoes shined. He refreshes him-self and after his pressed clothing arrives, dresses and awaits his return to Mrs. Norton's horse farm.

CHAPTER 7

Dinner Together

T he coach from the farm arrives, he extinguishes his pipe and enters for the short ride to Mrs. Norton's house. Upon arrival, he is escorted by Clarence, the butler, into the den, offered a sherry which he gladly accepts and awaits Mrs. Norton's arrival.

As she enters the room, Sherlock rises and greets her, "Good evening Mrs. Norton."

She gazes unblinkingly upon him and after momentary hesitation says, "Good evening Reginald. May I call you Reginald or Reggie?"

"Yes, without question, Reggie would be fine, Mrs. Norton."

Smiling she says "Please call me Irene, since we are such old friends."

She leads him to the Veranda, saying, "Dinner will be served soon, we may sit here since it is such a pleasant evening, you may finish drinking your sherry, and we will not be overheard since I told the staff to announce when dinner is ready."

She seats herself at a bench and indicates Holmes sit next to her.

She says, "I read about your demise in the New York newspapers, and I was very saddened you should come to such an untimely and gruesome end, and yet here you are. How?"

He smiles at her and starts his narrative on how he survived, "When Professor Moriarty and I met above the falls, and before we entered into our deadly combat, he vouchsafed to permit me to write my note to Watson since I firmly believed the only outcome of our combat would be my, his or our deaths. He was a very worthy opponent; our battle lasted several minutes which seemed like hours; finally, we were on the brink, and over we went. On the way down, I made purchase on an overhang; saw my antagonist plummet to his certain death in the rocky gorge below."

He pauses as he remembers the event, then he resumes, "I made my way back up to the rim of the gorge; rested for a moment when I saw a figure in the distance hastening towards the spot. I knew at once it was Watson; I instantly concluded I was better served to be dead since there were at least three others who wanted to take my life. I tried to ascend the rock wall but was almost hit by a falling rock, which did not fall but was hurled by one of those three, a companion of Moriarty. I eluded him and made my way to another town to communicate with my brother, Mycroft, seeking his help to keep me dead and supply me with needed funds until I could rid myself of these malevolent individuals."

He hesitated, and she interjects, "My word what an adventure, it makes the one I had very mild. Please go on, if you wish."

"I do, what transpired was a journey across Europe into Asia with some adventures on the way for nearly a year and a half, and while in contact with Mycroft, learned only one of my potential assassins was in London, the others being dispatched during the year. Once the burden was lifted, I made haste to the United States and to you, Irene."

"During my travels, I was aided by my brother, Mycroft, who supplied me with funds, passports, and new identities."

"Surely, there is more which transpired during the year?"

"Yes, there were other incidents, but I pray I will have more time to relate them to you over the next several years and beyond."

She laughs, interrupted by Clarence's deep voice announcing dinner is to be served.

Dinner is served to Mrs. Norton and Mr. Reginald Wallace, that night and for many more nights, which were interspersed around walks, carriage rides, theater presentations, charitable events, luncheons, horses, horse racing, and more about his exploits and his hidden life and her life after the crown prince, her sadness at the loss of her husband, and how she copes for the loss with her charity work and her stable of racing horses.

CHAPTER 8

Sherlock's Family History

One evening, after dinner, Irene says, "Reggie, I know very little of your life, other than the writings of Dr. John Watson, I would like to know more about you and your family."

Smiling she inquires. "Are you the offspring of a gang of villains, traveling gypsies, or a descendant of royalty? You say Mycroft is your brother, do you have other siblings?"

He stays silent for a short while and then begins. "I am the youngest of three sons of my parents, Serenity and Malcolm Holmes. My father died in 1869 in a hunting accident, leaving my mother a widow. My eldest brother is Arthur, who inherited the bulk of the small estate, and he and his wife, Elizabeth, my mother, and their four daughters live there."

"Arthur is a very bright and sound businessman; over the years has grown the estate into one of the most profitable in Northern England, keeping both Mycroft and me in sound financial position, which I have not used, but have Arthur keeping it for me should the need arise. You would like them, and I am certain you would like the nice stable of horses on the estate."

"Mycroft lives, as you know, in the Diogenes Club in London, has some high but undefined position in the British Government, possesses a keen analytical mind; prefers the solitary sedentary life, hardly ever venturing outside the club. During my dead period, he kept me in funds, passports, and abreast of what was happening in London. We used coded telegrams to converse."

"After university, and a halfhearted attempt to help with the estate, Arthur drew me aside one day saying, "You are too talented in what you do to stay here, there are not enough criminals locally, except for Bobby, whom you have caught six times stealing chickens, so I think you should join Mycroft in London, and use your skills to do something important."

"So, I left in '81 for London and began my career."

"Well," he continues, "now you know of my lineage. One thing, I neglected to tell you, no one, outside of Mycroft, knows what I have told you. I have kept Arthur and his family, a secret, since, one never knows if one of those I apprehended would try to take revenge on Arthur and his family."

She looks at him and says, "I feel pleased you confided in me."

CHAPTER 9

Irene's Life After Godfrey

O ver the course of the following weeks, Irene recalled the last year of Godfrey's life as he fought to ward off tuberculosis. They tried various climates, but in the end, it was not enough. She felt lost, took him home to England to be buried when it was done she was shunned by his family and she returned to America.

Sherlock learned Irene's family of mother, father, two sisters, and a brother live closer to New York. They are a solid and righteous group who while pleased with Irene's fame, are privately embarrassed by her antics abroad, her private wedding, and her flamboyance. In effect, they had severed all ties to her and had not seen her in several years.

She was saddened by this but buried this feeling in her many charitable works, and her horses. She had amassed a small fortune through her musical performances to live the life she has made for herself.

One afternoon, she recounted, to Sherlock, her family cut her off and she said, "I felt bad for years about Godfrey's death, and what my family has done to me, but with you here, I feel totally alive again for the first in many years. Thank you."

He says, "No, thank you, I feel the same."

CHAPTER 10

Proposal

November 19, 1982

I t has been three weeks since he arrived, and his feelings for her have grown more and more each day.

Sitting in the parlor with biscuits and freshly brewed tea, Irene says, "It has been nearly three years since my husband, Godfrey, perished from the disease. I have mourned enough and as you know I have never been restricted by the social graces or conventions, but I know nearly three years is enough time to satisfy even the busiest of busybodies. So what do your propose, and I use that word with its intended use, to do about my condition? I haven't much more time to spare."

Sherlock is befuddled, but finally says, "Irene will you be my wife?"

"Finally, you asked! I know you have been wanting to for so long, and my answer is yes, I'll become Mrs. Holmes or Mrs. Wallace, or Mrs. Whatever is to your liking."

"Mrs. Holmes it will be, but only between you and I, the minister and a trusted witness."

"The witness will be Clarence, the minister is a very dear friend and confidant, and when shall it be."

"As soon as we may arrange it."

"It has been arranged, only waiting on you, and we will wed the day after tomorrow."

And so they are wed, and after the private ceremony, a small party of the household staff, a few close friends of the now Mrs. Wallace, and the minister attend a wedding reception.

They leave the following day for a honeymoon trip to Niagara Falls, which neither of them had ever seen.

CHAPTER 11

Married Life

A fter the trip, they fall into a routine of charity events, horse racing, principally at Brighton Beach in Brooklyn New York, and Monmouth Park in Oceanport, New Jersey, a horse buying trip to Saratoga Race Course in Saratoga Springs, New York, attending theater in New York, trips to the New Jersey shore, reading, Sherlock playing his violin and Irene vocalizing, all in all, an idyllic life.

This continues until winter's end of 1892, when Irene says, "I have always wanted to have one of our horse's race at Churchill Downs in Louisville, Kentucky, and to be there for the annual May running of the Kentucky Derby. It is a race of one and one-half miles and showcases the best horses."

Sherlock looking up from his newspaper says, " That sounds like a nice trip, a second honeymoon. As you know, I have not been farther west in America than Niagara Falls."

"Well, it is settled, I will start making arrangements and see if we can have Bohemian Escape run in one of the lower class races since he is not championship material, but still a good horse that may do well against comparable competition."

He replies, "I agree; I am always amused by the horse's name Bohemian Escape. I look forward to the trip with grand expectations."

"I know that our lives have been wonderful, yet I sometimes see in your eyes a glimmer of looking back to your numerous successes in solving inexplicable crimes and you truly miss the chase."

"No, my dear I am quite happy and content."

"Well, maybe our trip to the Kentucky Derby will be as exciting as some of your previous adventures."

"I am certain that it will be an adventure, as is every day with you, my dear."

CHAPTER 12

The Kentucky Derby

May 6, 7, and 8, 1893

Irene makes the arrangements, they leave on Saturday, May the sixth on the ten AM train for the trip to Louisville.

They will be two days in transit traveling in a private suite, viewing the countryside of Pennsylvania, Ohio, and Kentucky before arriving in Louisville on May the eighth also at ten AM. The trip was enjoyable and they are full of anticipation for the Derby and having Bohemian Escape run in a race before the Derby.

As they prepare to leave the train, Irene says, "Reggie, I hope the Derby and our trip will be adventure enough to make you at ease."

Sherlock replies, "I am certain that it shall."

With that, they make certain the horse is taken care of and is in transit to Churchill Downs. They have their luggage sent onto the Galt House for their later arrival after securing Bohemian Escape in its stable for the duration of their visit to the Derby.

Once the horse is settled, they make way to the hotel, register, and get to their room to unpack and rest before venturing out into this Kentucky city. Irene has read that the current Galt House is the second to bear the name after the first was destroyed by fire in 1865. It is an elegant and larger version of the first on the northeast corner of First and Main Streets, near the Ohio River as many guests arrive by steamboat. The Galt House has the best accommodations for the largest and best parties in the city.

CHAPTER 13

Derby Preparations
May 9, 1893

On Tuesday, they have an early breakfast; go to the track to check on Bohemian Escape; speak to the jockey, Josiah Jackson, who will ride him the next day, watch his workout and after they are satisfied that everything is ready for the next day they settle into an owner's box to view the races placing wagers on their best guess of a winner.

Later in the afternoon, Irene says with a smile, "Darling, it is very good that you are a great detective because you are not a good handicapper of horses."

"Very true, I should have paid more attention to Watson when he would tell me about his wagering prowess and how he picked so many winners if indeed he did."

"Well, there are only two more races today, maybe we shall recoup our losses. If not, there is always tomorrow."

They leave the track both losing with Irene losing much less than Sherlock.

On the way to the hotel, Irene makes a stop at a milliner, whose name was given to her by the hotel staff, to buy a colorful hat for the Derby which is the required headwear for the ladies attending and is, supposedly, a good luck charm. Proper attire for the ladies is full morning dress. Once satisfied with her purchase they return to the hotel.

They rest and dress for dinner, which they decide they would have in the hotel since they want to be up early, breakfast and go to the track, check on Bohemian Escape, and get settled in the owners' box for an exciting day.

Little did they know how exciting.

A DEATH AT THE DERBY

CHAPTER 1

Discovery

May 10, 1893

10 AM

I rene and Sherlock arise early on Wednesday morning, have breakfast in their suite, and prepare for an exciting day at Churchill Downs and the Kentucky Derby. Once dressed for the track, she in her new lucky Derby hat, they leave the Galt House and take a carriage arriving at the track by ten, and enter the track through the owners' entrance. They make their way to the stables, with Irene viewing with excitement the seemingly orchestrated pandemonium. They continue until they are outside the stable housing Bohemian Escape, he is a fine horse but as they draw near his stall, he is extremely excited, not his normal subdued self who just patiently waits for the race, conserving his energy. Irene enters the stall and tries to calm the horse but to no avail.

Sherlock, as is his nature, knows something is amiss and looks into Escape's stall sees nothing out of the ordinary, as Irene continues to soothe the horse. He checks the adjoining stalls which have no horses in them, the one to the left is empty but the one on the right is surprisingly occupied by what appears to be a very dead well dressed middle-aged man, lying face down in the non mucked stall.

10:10 AM

Before entering the stall, he calls out to Irene asking her to leave Escape and come to him. She hesitates not wanting to leave the horse but leaves going to her husband.

Following his gaze, she sees the dead man and she is repelled, but soon gathers herself.

"He is dead isn't he?"

"Very, please find someone to fetch a constable and have him return immediately."

She hurries off in pursuit of help in finding a police officer.

Investigation

Holmes enters the stall cautiously and carefully so as not to disturb the scene. He scrutinizes the area adjacent to the body and finds two sets of footsteps, not three. Neither is the size of the dead man's feet, nor the style of his shoes. Those footprints entering the stall are more recessed into the soil and straw of the stall while those leaving are not as depressed as the others, meaning the two sets of footsteps brought in the dead man, whose shoe soles are unmarked by the floor of the stall's unclean covering, and from all indications the body was flung down, not laid down, as it, like the incoming footsteps is deep in the soil and straw.

He carefully withdraws from the stall and examines the soil outside, follows the inward and outward trail of the two bearers of the dead man.

Irene arrives telling him, a groom is on the way to find a constable.

"Irene please keep watch on the stall and keep out anyone who might have an interest in entering while I follow the trail of the men who brought this man here."

He follows the footsteps of the two men to an intersecting lane where he loses the footsteps in the heavily traveled path.

Holmes makes one more observation, of a wagon that had one wheel with a notch on the inside of the wheel and the wagon had been stationary for sometime before moving. Based on the difference between the front and rear wheels, the wagon was a standard freight size. The ingress and regress footprints of the carriers both vanish at this wagon. With nothing more to be learned he returns to the stall where the dead man lay.

Irene is glad he returned, and Sherlock venturing closer, feels the man's face which is well below normal body temperature and more in keeping with the outside temperature, therefore he has been dead for several hours, probably deposited hours earlier. Since the dead man is face down, Holmes could not see whether there are any wounds to explain the cause of death.

The dead man's suit is well-tailored in an English fashion, his shoes are well made, probably Italian evidenced by the use of patent leather. His left arm lays under his face with the hand visible beyond his head and bears a ring with the emblem of the Masons.

The men who brought the body into the stall based upon the length of their stride were very different in size. Man number one has a thirty-inch stride meaning he stands six feet tall, and based upon the depth of the receding footsteps weighs 168 pounds, while the other man has a twenty-six-inch stride and is smaller with a height of five foot three inches and weighs approximately 175 pounds. Man number one is thin for his height while man number two is rotund and walks with a limp favoring his right leg.

Leaning near the corpse's head, he sniffs the air and finds a trace of Kentucky bourbon, but no tobacco odor, touching the man's coat collar and lowering it slightly, he sees bruises which might mean the man had been strangled. Replacing the collar as he found it.

As he is retreating, he spies tobacco ash on one of the stables crossbars, and he pulls a small envelope from his inside pocket and brushes the ash into it for future reference. He carefully extracts himself from the stall and waits for the constable, and with Irene guards the stall preserving the scene.

CHAPTER 3

Police Arrive

10:25 AM

Within minutes, a groom returns with two men, one a uniformed constable, named Hammersmith, and the other a police Captain, Harvey Williams.

The Captain barks at his constable, "I come to spend a peaceful day at the track and I am not amused to be drawn away from my friends for what is probably some female exaggeration. If there is indeed a dead man, he probably died of natural causes."

He shouts, "Where is the corpse?"

Holmes says, "Over here, sir."

As the Captain approaches the stall where Holmes stands, he tries to move around Holmes. Who stays steadfast in front of the stall.

Captain grumpily says, "Who are you?"

My name is Reginald Wallace and this is my wife, Mrs. Irene Wallace."

Captain says without enthusiasm, "Grand to meet you, now get out my way man, and what is this about a dead man?"

Holmes does not move but replies, "I'm certain my wife was succinct enough for you to grasp there is indeed a dead man in the stall behind me."

" Well, let's have a look at the corpse," and proceeds to attempt to pass Holmes for the second time to enter the stall.

Holmes blocks his way again, saying "Captain, please be aware there is evidence in the stall to confirm what I have found, but if you and your constable stumble in, you will definitely trod on the evidence I have seen."

Captain Williams grows agitated at this lanky Englishman standing in his way, saying "What are you talking about?"

"There are recent footmarks in the stall which do not belong to the dead man, he did not walk into the stall alive, but was carried in and dumped rather harshly into the uncleaned stall by two men."

"How do you know this, were you here or did you do it?"

Holmes sighs and replies, "It was my observation of the scene based upon my years of assisting the local constabulary in my native England."

Captain inquires, "Are you a policeman?"

"No, but I am a member of the Queen's secret service, and have been involved in solving numerous criminal acts."

The Captain eyes him suspiciously and says, "So you say, we'll have to verify that, now may I enter carefully so as not to damage your supposed precious evidence?"

10:30 AM
Holmes steps aside allowing the Captain to enter and watches as the Captain carefully examines the scene noting three sets of footsteps.

He says, "You said two sets of footmarks, there are three."

"Yes, the third set around the body is mine, and the others are those of the two transporters of the dead man." "

"Oh, I see."

CHAPTER 4

Victim Identified

T he dead man is turned over onto his back and the Captain exclaims, "I will be damned, I know this man it is Albert Vincent, finally, someone has done him in."

The Captain retreats and compares his observations with those made by Holmes and they match with a little discrepancy. Holmes shows the Captain the ingress and regress footprints of the men until they vanished in the lane. They coincidentally disappear at the point where the wagon with the marked wheel sat for a time.

The Captain says, "Vincent did not die from natural causes, but seems to have been strangled."

Irene watches and listens to the interchange between her husband and the Captain with great interest.

10:45AM
Holmes standing next to Irene addresses the Captain saying, "It would be most appreciated if one of the constables could have a suitable carriage brought round to take my wife to the Galt House since this has been a most stressful event for her to witness."

Irene nudges Holmes and is about to speak when he winks at her and shakes his head ever so slightly, and she does not speak but is dismayed. The Captain agrees and has a constable speak to a young lad to make haste to arrange for a carriage.

Holmes says, "You say you knew the victim but you do not seem surprised by his murder?"

"Yes, unfortunately, I did know him, and I am not surprised someone killed him. For your information, Vincent was a

Mason, an unmarried womanizer with a handsome appearance and suave nature. That is as far as good points go. He was a small-time horseman, police informant, gambler, and purveyor of salacious information about well-positioned people in Kentucky, Ohio, and Indiana. He had been arrested numerous times but was never convicted since those involved were reluctant to come forward. His status as a horseman was achieved when he won a three-year-old colt, Abe's Legacy, in a card game with its owner, Henry Johnson, a very small time horseman and a worse card player who possesses a very volatile personality which he had violently used on occasion especially if he thought he had been cheated or swindled. Albert frequented many high society events but since he wasn't a member of high society, it was uncertain how he got his invitations to these events. He was a member of the prestigious Masonic Lodge, and his invitations may have come from a member of the lodge. Anyone of his avocations might have brought him to his end, but we have settled on Henry Johnson, he of the violent nature and loser mentality."

"Quite an unsavory individual with many potential enemies. Well, do not let me hinder you more in your investigation."

CHAPTER 5

Contact London

As the Captain continues his perusal of the scene. Holmes and Irene walk away from him, and once out of earshot, Holmes says, "My dear, I know you are not dismayed, but I need you to return to the hotel and make contact with Mycroft, in code of course, instructing him that he is to elevate my pseudonym of Reginald Wallace to a sufficient rank in the Queen's Secret Service before the Inspector makes his inquiry"

She looks at him and smiles impishly saying, "My you are the devious one, using my so-called feminine sensitivity to cover an act of deceit upon the nice Captain. I'll do my daintiest best to accommodate your ruse, my love." He returns her smile caressing her arm ever so lovingly in deep appreciation.

Holmes and Irene watch the Captain marshal his troop of constables, increasing by the minute, and he assigns each to make inquiries of the workers, jockeys, exercise boys, track officials, and anyone else loitering about.

11 AM
The carriage arrives and Irene leaves with an upset look on her face, not upset about the murder, but upset that she has to leave.

CHAPTER 6

Culprits Identified

T he inquiries continue through the morning with very little pertinent information gathered until an exercise boy who had spent the better part of the night and morning with a cantankerous horse is questioned. He says he noticed a wagon with two men, one tall and one short with the taller one thinner than the other, who was fatter. They were leaving the stable area around six in the morning and appeared to be in a hurry. He did not know either man or saw anything unusual about the wagon. He said the small fat man had a full beard, and the tall man sported a mostly gray mustache. They left by the West lane, headed out the main road, and then turned North, then he said he lost interest and went to get breakfast.

The county coroner had been summoned earlier, arrives, examines the body, and concludes Vincent had indeed been strangled and died at approximately four o'clock in the morning.

He said, "I'll know more after the autopsy."

Vincent's body is loaded into a hearse for transfer to the morgue. The Captain and his constables conclude their inquiries into the murder at the race track and head back to the police station before the first race of the day. Before departing, the Captain finds Holmes and informs him the police are heading back to the police station to create a case file based upon the results of their inquiries.

The Captain says, "Are you staying at the Galt House, Mr. Wallace?"

"Yes we are, we plan to watch the Derby, we had a horse running in an earlier race, but being so upset, we will probably pull him from the race today. If there is anything I could do to help,

I would greatly appreciate the diversion if it would forestall a sightseeing trip, going to the theater, or worse. I am trying mightily to adjust to my state of being recently married."

Of course, this was untrue, but Holmes was attempting to appeal to another man's lack of interest in pastimes which were not the activities men of action preferred.

The Captain smiles slightly and says, "Well, myself not being married, Mr. Wallace, I can still sympathize with you. I may call upon you at the Galt House later tomorrow to let you know what we have learned."

"Thank you for your courtesy and I look forward to seeing you tomorrow. Good day."

Holmes leaves the stable area, employs a coach, and heads to the Galt House to meet, he was certain, a mildly upset Irene.

CHAPTER 7

Irene's Business

1:00 PM

Entering their hotel room, he finds Irene writing in her diary, she pauses, closes the diary, rises, goes to her husband, embraces him and kisses him.

She says, "How was the rest of your police inquiries? Did you apprehend the murderer? If so, I assume we can continue with our itinerary?"

He smiles and laughing replies, "Good, no, and maybe."

"Well, that is rather succinct."

Smiling, she continues, "Tell me all about it."

He proceeds to bring her up to date and to say he might be called to assist the police in their investigations. She is surprised, not that he might be asked, but that the Captain offered it.

Sherlock sheepishly admits he had appealed to the Captain as one man to another that he would relish helping the police as opposed to some other tasks, like sightseeing, the theater, or other pursuits, his wife enjoys. She should be upset but is amused by his ploy to squeeze into the investigation.

She says" While you idled about at the stalls waiting for the police to complete their inquiries, I was very busy. First back to the hotel, sending off the coded request to Mycroft and then back to the track office withdrawing Bohemian Escape from the day's race card. I asked if I might be able to enter Bohemian Escape in a race tomorrow. I left there with an assurance they would do all they could to accommodate my request, and they would let me know by the end of the day, and lastly, before leaving the track I placed a five-dollar wager on Lookout to win the

Derby."

"I almost forgot while at the track office, we received an invitation from the track officials to attend a gala at Galt House, this evening following the races, and we have accepted."

She was certain Sherlock would be eager to attend since much of the evening's talk would be about the murder at the Derby. Undoubtedly, she, a famous singer would be a most welcome guest.

They were both up to date and decide to return to the track. Since there was nothing more to do about the murder except await more information from the Captain.

So they go to Churchill Downs for the Derby and a small late lunch.

They watch Lookout win the Derby by four lengths ridden by Jockey Eddie Kunze. Irene was elated she won $8.50 on her $5.00 bet.

As they are leaving the track, Irene collects her winnings, they hire a carriage to return to the hotel, but on the way, Holmes asks the driver to take them to the police station.

Irene is somewhat surprised and inquires, "Why the police station?"

"I would like to find out what progress has been made in the case."

CHAPTER 8

Police Update

A rriving at the police station, Holmes asks to see the Captain.

Within minutes they are escorted to his office. The Captain is surprised to see them, but pleased. He tells them they are looking into all leads, but the case file grows with no apparent end in sight.

The Captain says, "My main suspect, Henry Johnson, is currently in jail in Indiana for drunkenness and a barroom fight, and has been in jail since Saturday night. But we have identified the ones who brought his Vincent's body to the stall based on your observations and those of the track lad, they are Percy Thornton, known as Thorn, and Davey Wonder, known as Donder. They are pals We are now hunting for them and we should have them soon. When we do, they will more than likely be the killers. Other than them, we have no other suspects.

Holmes, "That is very good news, and I look forward to meeting them."

"If Vincent's murder is not enough, early this morning, a young prostitute was found in an alley near the brothels with her throat cut. A nasty business, but violence is often a part of that profession."

Holmes quizzically asks, "Her throat cut?"

"Yes, but it has no bearing on the Vincent killing, so what may I do for you?"

"Nothing more, I am just interested in the progress you have made. Good afternoon."

Once complete at the station, they return to the hotel and dress for an early supper before attending the Gala.

Irene has a message from the track informing her that Bohemian Escape may run tomorrow in the third race for a horse that has been scratched, but they need a reply immediately. She calls the track and says Escape will run tomorrow. She asks them to contact her jockey and a groom to have Escape ready for the race. She is elated.

After dinner, they take a sightseeing carriage ride around the city before heading back to the hotel for the Gala.

Sherlock and Irene look forward to a fruitful evening.

CHAPTER 9

THE DERBY GALA

7:00 PM

T he Gala is in full swing when Sherlock and Irene arrived.

Irene with her past well known is beseeched to entertain with her outstanding voice. She gives an impressive performance which has all attendees entranced.

She is also engaged in talking about her removal of Bohemian Escape from the race at the downs, because the poor horse was so upset, but she looks forward to him racing tomorrow.

Irene dances with almost every man in attendance.

While all of this is transpiring, Holmes, acting the overshadowed husband by his wife's fame, is involved in light conversation with many of the attendees.

Holmes listens and inquires about topics that are brought up as he passes from group to group of men.

He is greeted by a couple of men, Mr. Andrew Nichols and Mr. Charles Wilson.

Nichols is a young man of average height with soft features, and a nervous tick in his left eye, he seems to be winking at you when he is not. He is far from being sober.

Wilson is a big man in all sizes, weighing in excess of two hundred fifty pounds, walks with a limp, and is quite bald.

Mr. Wilson introduces himself saying, "Your wife gave a superb performance and it was greatly appreciated by all in attendance. Is it true you found the body of Vincent?"

"Yes, regrettably so."

"How frightful for Mrs. Wallace."

"Yes, it was, but Irene is a very strong lady and no doubt will be fine."

Wilson continues, "Vincent was not well-liked, but not being liked is no reason to kill him."

All three agree, and Nichols who is quite inebriated says, "He was a bounder, and more, he will not be missed by anyone. Worse yet is the vile way the young prostitute was murdered, much less deserving of killing than Vincent."

Jestingly he says, "Her demise is certainly a waste of a pretty young thing."

Wilson sharply rebukes him saying, "Prostitution is an evil practice, but despite that, the death of any young woman should be mourned and not be the subject of an unseemly attempt at humor."

Nichols says, "I apologize, it is the drink. I did not mean to make light of the girl, Evelyn's death. I am so, so sorry."

Wilson gently takes Nichols by the arm and leads him away, saying to Holmes, "I need to take care of him." As Nichols stumbles away, supported by Wilson.

After they leave, Holmes walks around and is summoned by a group of four men, Mr. Gilbert Thompson, Dr. Richard Jones, Colonel John Hawthorne, and retired General Wellington.

Dr. Jones, a short thin man possessing a full head of red hair and sporting very thick glasses.

Mr. Thompson appears to be very fit, handsome, with a bull neck and long black hair down to his shoulders.

Colonel Hawthorne's appearance is of a fit military man exceeding six feet in height, a well-trimmed beard and mustache of brown hair, and an overbearing presence.

Last, is the General, who in his earlier years must have had an erect posture, but the years have not been good to him, he is now stooped, unsteady on his feet, his full beard is sprinkled with gray, and wears a wig and gloves.

The General says, "Mr. Wallace, you are truly graced to be married to such a wonderfully talented wife."

"Yes, I am very graced, but sometimes I feel greatly and rightfully overshadowed by Irene's glow."

Dr. Jones, "Yes, I can see that, but I've been told that it was you who discovered the dead Mr. Vincent in the horse stall."

"That is somewhat correct, Irene and I found him, Bohemian Escape, Irene's horse was quite upset by something, which we believe was the body of the poor fellow."

General retorted, "Poor fellow, eh? He was a bounder, cheat, and philander, and only the Lord knows how much else. He will not be missed by anyone except the women of the red light district. But Thompson wasn't he a friend of yours?"

Mr. Thompson replies, "Yes he was and he was not all bad."

Colonel Hawthorne says, "But, he had a well deserved poor reputation."

Holmes says,"Well, that might shed some light on the reason for his surprising departure."

The Colonel responds,"Well said, he may have been surprised, but I think he spent a good amount of time watching his back."

The General sees a woman waving to him and he excuses himself and says,"Good talking with you Mr., er Mr. Walker", and hobbles across the ballroom to meet with a woman, later identified by Irene as Mrs. Vivian Singleton.

Dr. Jones says after the General leaves, "You must excuse the General's forgetfulness concerning your name, he sometimes has memory lapses, but it is nothing serious."

Holmes responds lightly, "Not a problem since I sometimes seem to forget my own name."

The three men stay with Wallace, and the conversation centers on Wallace.

The Colonel asks, "I understand you are helping Captain Williams with the investigation of Vincent's murder, is that correct?"

"Yes, I do what little I may, feeling somewhat involved after finding Vincent."

Thompson says, "I understand from my sources, you have done more than a little in the investigation, but have helped the police move in the right direction. Are you a trained policeman?"

"I have some experience in police work in my native England, and I help where I may."

With that the conversation lags and the men drift apart.

CHAPTER 10

Bartender's Insight

A fter He is left alone, he finds a bar and orders a gin n' tonic from the bartender, who wears a name tag with Alfie on it. Alfie has a lull in business asks him, "Are you English, sir?

"Yes, Alfie, I am. And you are from Scotland, are you not?"

"Yes, but times being what they are in the old country, I decided to move to the States, and give up my kilt."

"So you are new to Louisville?"

"No sir, I have been here near five years and very pleased with the country."

"When you come back I have a few questions?"

"Yes sir, I will get your drink and be right back."

Alfie comes back with the drink and says, "Now how may I help you, sir?"

"I have met a number of men tonight, and I would like to know more about them."

"I will do my best, sir."

"I hope I have their names correct, First, Dr. Jones is he a physician?"

"No, he is a university president, unmarried, lucky bloke, his a mighty high impression of himself and sees right through people like me."

"Next, Colonel Hawthorne."

"He is a Civil War hero, they say, lawyer and was something in the government."

"Andrew Nichols."

"Now there is a chap, he is a bartender's best friend, always drinking too much, but generous with his tips, does not work, his family is rich and he is always looking for a good or better time. Excuse me I have to fill some trays for the guests."

Alfie returns, Holmes says, "Next is Charles Wilson."

"Yes, he made a fortune out west during the gold rush and has made even more after, is an art dealer, and does not have to sell much to keep himself. I heard he had some bad time but was saved by a Mr. Henderson, a lay preacher."

"General Wellington."

"A retired Union General has a lot of money, well respected, but some say he is not well."

"Gilbert Thompson"

"He owns a local newspaper which publishes racy stories about many people, if you want dirt and gossip about someone he is the person to see. I heard, he was a friend of Mr. Vincent, the one killed at the track, today. Any more?"

Holmes mentions two others, they are not truly in high society.

"Alfie, you have been most helpful."

He gives him a generous tip and says goodbye.

He sees Irene being whirled around the dance floor by some heavy-footed and uncoordinated man. She is being courteous, but he can see she is not having a very good time.

CHAPTER 11

Ladies of the Gala

H e stops and watches the festivities of the gala when he is tapped on the shoulder by a young woman and as he turns he finds himself facing not one, but four ladies. They are Mrs. Atkinson, Miss Carson, Mrs. Ambrose, and Mrs. Singleton.

Mrs. Atkinson is of medium height for a lady, dresses flamboyantly and has large blue eyes that are always searching for something.

Miss Carson is much younger than the other ladies. She is attractive with a thin figure and a heart-shaped smiling face which seemingly appears to be laughing either with you or about you.

Mrs. Ambrose is a stout woman of medium height dressed in black, and a round face with sad-looking eyes.

Mrs. Singleton is a sturdy looking woman with black hair tinged with gray and seems to be amused by almost anything.

Almost at once, they all begin to speak, stopping to introduce themselves.

Holmes acknowledges each courteously and expresses how much this gala has meant to Irene, and of course to himself.

Miss Carson speaks first saying, "I know you and your wife found the body of Mr. Vincent, how dreadful for you both, and your first impression of our fine city is a murder."

The other three ladies nod in agreement.

Holmes replies solemnly, " Yes, it was a shock, but we were pleased that those responsible for the murder were not present when we found him. We do not judge your fine city on the scurrilous actions of others."

Mrs. Ambrose sighs and says, "Thank you. We understand you are assisting the police with this matter."

"Yes, I am doing what little I can to assist the police."

Mrs. Singleton queries, "Are you a policeman, or just an interested bystander?"

"My background before coming to the United States was in law enforcement, so whatever I can do to help, I will do so if asked."

Miss Carson says, " Albert may be missed by some, but not by many, so don't try too hard to find the killer because he did us all a favor."

Holmes does not tell them that those involved in the killing of Vincent are identified and being hunted.

Mrs. Singleton angrily replies, "Natalie, you are very disrespectful of the dead, he will be judged by the good Lord and not by us."

Natalie Carson retorts, "If the Lord does it right, Vincent is shaking hands with Satan."

Mrs. Atkinson, who had not spoken before shakily replies, "That's enough. You are tarnishing Mr. Wallace's opinion of us and our city."

With that she turned to Holmes and says, "Our apologies for this outburst,
please forgive us."

He quietly says " Think nothing of it" and then the ladies say their goodbyes and depart.

After his session with the women, Holmes goes back to the same bartender, Alfie, for another gin n' tonic, and more information, this time about the women he spoke with. He had dumped his first drink into a potted plant.

"Alfie, I am back for another drink and, if you may help, more information. I have met so many people tonight I can not seem to keep them straight, maybe it is the gin."

"Sir, these parties are too noisy and loud, to keep anything straight. I will make your drink and be right back."

"Thank you."

Holmes-like the last time will throw in a couple of names of people who are not of interest to him.

Alfie returns and Holmes says, "Maybe you could help me, again. I would like to know more about some of the people I have met tonight, they seem so nice for instance, Mrs. Ambrode, Miss Carton, Mrs. Singlely, Mrs. Atconson, Mrs. Beally, and a Mrs. Chester."

Alfie laughs and says, "You have all their names jumbled up.

The first is Mrs. Ambrose, she is wealthy, owns a bourbon distillery, a widow, and always wears black for her dead husband, who died, I heard, some twenty years ago.

Miss Carson is an heiress to a furniture fortune, outspoken and attractive, if I may say.

Mrs. Singleton owns an iron supply company, a widow with no offspring, and a member of the high society.

Mrs. Atkinson owns a railway, a genteel lady, dresses flamboyantly, but is a sly business person.

You got the last two correct, Mrs. Beally and Mrs. Chester are sisters, and both are married, Mr. Beally works for the railroad and Mr. Chester works for a bank. They are not as well to do as the others. I know nothing else about them, sir."

Holmes replies, "How could I have had all of their names so misunderstood. I thank you for your insight, and thank you for the drink, and here is a nice tip for you."

"Thank you very much, you break the mold of all Englishmen, being tight with money and scornful of Scots."

"May your next encounter with an Englishman, be as beneficial. Thank you and goodnight."

As Holmes is leaving, the bartender says, "If you need any more information, I would be happy to assist."

"If I need more insight, Alfie, I shall be back."

As Holmes walks around the ballroom, he overhears some chatter about Vincent, but nothing to draw his attention, he sees Irene is not being dragged around the dance floor, he hurries over and catches her before she may find a seat.

He asks, "May I have this dance, my dear?"

"Yes, but you must promise not to step on my poor feet."

"I will do my best since as you know I am a novice at dancing."

"Have you learned anything?"
"I think I have, how about you?"

"I have learned that many of these men do not know how to dance, and that they are all interested in Mr. Vincent's demise, and a substantial number of them think it was long overdue."

They continue their dance in amiable silence, and when the music stops, Holmes says, "I will see you later."

Leaving her momentarily alone until a shy young man approaches and asks if she would dance with him. She replies, "Yes of course."

CHAPTER 12

Irene, Bell of the Gala

A bandoned by her husband, Irene continues to be the queen of the ball with almost all of the men in attendance. She can not keep track of all the men she danced with. Most are interested in her discovery of the dead Mr. Vincent, but none referred to him as poor Mr. Vincent, they are pleased she had not been too distressed to miss the gala.

While taking a break from the dancing, she finds a waiter, picks a glass of wine off the tray he holds, and heads for the balcony to get some fresh air since the ballroom is heavy with the smell of cigars and cigarettes. As she pauses, sips her wine in a secluded part of the balcony, she hears two men talking in lowered voices.

One man says, "Kane, we must not be hasty, this man, Wallace, is making the Captain pursue other leads."

Kane says, "We cannot let this go on much longer, it is dangerous."

The other says, "Lucas, be patient, it will all work out."

They say no more and leave the balcony exiting through another door. Before Irene dares to look, they are gone, and then her dancing merry-go-round starts again.

She dances with Mr. Andrew Nichols, who is very inebriated and does not dance well but keeps up an ongoing conversation with her, and he has a very low opinion of the deceased Mr. Vincent. He says, "Vincent got what he deserved, some would say, he deserved it, but not Evelyn, the young prostitute who was also found murdered today. Oh, I am so sorry I brought her killing up."

Thankfully, she is saved from more of Mr. Nichols by Dr. Richard Jones, who cuts in freeing her from Nichols' grasp.

The Dr. says,"I hope Andrew, Mr. Nichols, did not upset you with his talk about murders. But I assume you must have been quite disturbed by your discovery of Vincent. Dr. Freud indicates such a shock may be suppressed but later on the shock is brought forth."

"I hope this is not the case, but frankly I have put it behind me."

She continues," I am more interested in the death of a young prostitute and cannot understand why no one has been brought to justice for such a vile action."

"Ladies should not dwell on the demise of a poor young woman, but put their minds to more agreeable matters and leave to the men who are better equipped to handle violent matters."

She responds, " I am certain that you are right." Not believing it for a moment.

The dance ends and she quickly leaves the dance floor looking for a place to sit. Once seated, she is quickly surrounded by Mrs. Veronica Atkinson, Miss Carson, Mrs. Ambrose, and Mrs. Singleton, all of whom introduce themselves.

They are all so happy Irene had graciously entertained them. Irene says it was her pleasure. The ladies feel her presence and bearing has raised the level of the gala, many of which result in too much drinking and loud bad behavior.

Mrs. Ambrose asks" Are you fully recovered from the shock of finding poor Mr. Vincent?"

That was the first time she had heard poor as a description of Vincent.

"Yes, I have recovered fully and am having a grand time at the gala meeting so many fine people."

Mrs. Atkinson says, "That is so kind of you. We all hope that you will not have a bad impression of our fine city."

"I do not think the demise of Mr. Vincent has made me possess a negative feeling about this fair city nor its citizens."

Mrs. Ambrose says, "I am so glad that you feel that way. If you have any anxieties about this whole sordid business, I can recommend you let me contact Professor Kane, and he may be able to relieve them. He has done so much for me, helping me get over the loss of my beloved husband."

Irene knows Kane is one of the men she overheard.

"Is he a physician?"

"No, no, my dear, he is a spiritualist with great insight. He is here tonight and I will ask him to call you at the hotel, and arrange an appointment if that is alright with you?"

"Mrs. Ambrose, you are so kind. Please have the professor call me, and make an appointment. Thank you"

"You are very welcome, and I think it may help with hidden worries."

The conversation stops, but Irene continues, "Did you know Mr. Vincent?"

They all nod, but Miss Carson interjects, "Mr. Vincent was not a member of our society, but an outsider trying to get in, but we would not allow one of such character to be part of our group."

Mrs. Atkinson retorts, " Natalie, it is not well mannered to speak ill of the dead."

Miss Carson replies, "His death does not improve the life he lived nor heal the wounds he made on far too many of us."

Mrs. Atkinson says, "Although there has been much gossip about Mr. Vincent's activities, nothing has been proven, but we all know he was said to be a frequent visitor to some illicit enterprises. But enough of airing dirty linen in front of our esteemed guest."

Irene looking over Mrs. Atkinson's shoulder sees a man talking to Dr. Jones and asks, "Who is that gentlemen talking to Dr. Jones?"

"Why do you ask?"

"He is probably the only man who has not danced with me."

Mrs. Ambrose says, "Well, that is Professor Lucas Kane, the man I told you about."

Irene responds, "A professor of what discipline?"

Mrs. Atkinson replies, "The occult, the supernatural and spiritualism. Some people think he is great while others think him to be charlatan, I do not profess to have any interest in what he is pedaling."

Mrs. Ambrose irritatingly responds, "Veronica, do not be so dismissive of the Professor, I have made considerable use of his powers over the years, and he has helped me over many hard times."

Mrs. Atkinson says, "I apologize Gloria for my insensitivity."

After a little more talk of less sensitive matters, the topic turns to horses, the gala, and the lovely city. The ladies say their goodbyes to Irene, and she starts searching for her husband.

She finds him having a conversation with a member of the wait staff. When he sees her, he bids farewell to the waiter and joins Irene, and heads for their room in silence.

CHAPTER 13

Hotel Suite Searched

O nce in their room, they are about to reveal what they had learned, but Sherlock makes Irene pause and whisks her into the bathroom.

After turning on the water in the tub, he whispers to her, "Our room has been professionally searched. Certain of my traps have been sprung. The hair over the side of the suitcase is no longer there, but on the floor and there are slight scratches on its lock."

He continues, "Evidently someone is interested in what Wallace knows and who he is."

In silence, Sherlock searches as the intruder did and finds everything was where it should be although slightly askew. He continues the search of the suite looking for possible listening posts.

His scrutiny is directed to the telephone which sits upon the desk in the suite's sitting room. The telephone is hooked up to the hotel's switchboard and could be used to connect with others in the Louisville area.

Sherlock's brilliant mind is much attuned to the world of science and he has studied the telephone's growth and technology and is very familiar with the mechanics of the device. His review of the desk telephone discloses a variation in the normal wiring. He quietly and expertly takes the telephone apart and finds that it has been modified, the device is always on and sending sound from the suite to someone else.

In effect, there are two telephones in the suite, one tied to the hotel's switchboard and one which is only a receiver wired to another phone or switchboard. The hidden telephone hookup would have to be found, traced to the other end to find those responsible.

Satisfied that he has done all that he could, enters the bathroom where Irene has been waiting patiently. Goes to the tub in the bathroom, and turns off the water running into the tub, but begins to run water into the sink.

He speaks quietly to her, "My dear, we are being spied upon by the desk telephone, it has been modified so anything we say will be overheard by some unknown person in an unknown location. They are very interested in what we are doing and what we know about the murder."

"What is this, we cannot be private in our hotel suite! You must notify the Captain and the hotel immediately!"

"Not now, tomorrow will do, we can just have casual conversation for the rest of the night."

Irene asks, "Alright, why the running water and the whispers?"

"The water makes it impossible to hear us clearly, and the whispering is so I may be closer to you."

"How romantic of you!"

Sherlock, "At least we know someone is nervous, they think we must be on to them."

Irene says, "Before you leave, I must tell you about the conversation I overheard from a Mr. Lucas Kane and another man."

She proceeds to tell him word for word what she had heard of the conversation, and what transpired when she asked the ladies who he might be.

Irene continues, "By the way, before I forget, Mrs. Ambrose is going to have Mr. Kane call me to arrange a visit with him to relieve my anxieties."

Sherlock laughs and says, "What anxieties?"

"I have none my dear, but I thought it might be good to meet him and see what kind of charlatan he is, and it may help the investigation in light of the snippet of conversation I overheard."

"That is very, very interesting. I think it might be most interesting to hear what he has to say, so by all means make an appointment with him. I do not think you will be in any danger, but in case do not eat or drink anything that he offers."

"Alright, and since we have a full tub, I think I shall bathe, please excuse me.'

"Certainly, now take your bath and I hope it refreshes you and heals your sore feet. While you bathe, I will play my violin and soothe our unseen eavesdropper's anxieties."

Sherlock retreats to the sitting room recalls his findings from his conversations with the men and women he spoke with at the gala, and what Irene overheard. As he does this, he thinks of the occupations of those people he and Irene had met and their many business interests, and which of them may have the wherewithal to break into their hotel room and set up the elaborate listening device.

Vincent had been murdered because of something he knew about someone, who could not submit to exposure.

Cheating at cards and winning a racehorse would not rise to a carefully planned killing, but would be a crime of rage. The loser, Henry Johnson, would not hire thugs to dispose of the body. The dumping of the body at the track may have been done to throw suspicion on Mr. Johnson. Evidently, they didn't know Johnson was in jail in Indiana.

An angered husband, suitor or family member could be the culprit, and it could be a family doing the deed, but hiring others to move the body would put them in jeopardy. Not a suitable option.

Sherlock thinks, where does this leave me? It does not seem to be revenge for a threat of revealed infidelity or past cheating at cards, but it still could be. But the former offenses could be handled by a severe beating and promises that more would come, but Vincent had not been beaten, just summarily dealt a quick death.

So if not the former, it must be something he knew and could prove, which would not only embarrass, but destroy the person or person or persons he was threatening with disclosure.

What could be so bad as to result in the cold-blooded killing of Vincent?

What about the killing of the prostitute?

Irene has bathed and is ready for a restful night's sleep for herself and her feet.

Tomorrow is another day, and possibly an interesting one.

CHAPTER 14

Police Summons

May 11 Thursday

10 AM

T he following morning after breakfast a hotel page brings a message from Captain Williams, and Holmes is called from his hotel to the police station to be taken to a scene related to the death of Vincent.

Once at the station, Holmes goes to see the police Captain, and before he speaks signals him to be silent and hands him a note explaining what is going on, and at once the Captain nods understanding. They leave the office, going to the park across the street.

Holmes explains what he found in his hotel room, seeks the Captain's help in finding the listening post of his suite, and suggests that the Captain check his phone to see if it is also being spied upon, but be careful not to say much in his office.

Holmes, "Whoever is listening is trying to gather unreleased information about the Vincent murder."

"If they were listening in my office, that is how they found out about the thugs who moved Vincent's body. I, by God, told them."

The Captain continues, "We have found them, but unfortunately they are both dead."

"As I suspected they would be."

Holmes continues, "Do you know a trustworthy person to who may check the telephone in my suite and find out where it leads which may aid us in catching the listener, red-handed.?"

"I will do that right now." He goes back to the station with Holmes following. Wallace waits at the police station entrance.

The Captain returns and says to Holmes, "The task is underway."

The Captain seems to have a better appreciation of Wallace's skills after he received a confirmation telegram of Wallace's excellence as an investigator from England via Mycroft.

CHAPTER 15

Murder Scene

10:30

O utside the station, a carriage is waiting for them. Holmes travels from the station with the Captain to the scene of the murders of the thugs on the bank of the Ohio River in a secluded heavily treed cove not visible from a nearby roadway.

Holmes is told the bodies were found early this morning by some young boys who were going fishing instead of going to school, they immediately went for a constable, who after some persuasion by the boys followed them to the spot. Convinced what the boys told him was true, he immediately sent the boys to the station for help. The constable was conscious of the need not to trample the area since there might be evidence related to the crime.

These were the men, Thorn and Davey, the ones identified as the two toughs who threw Vincent into the stall. They had reputations as robbers, thieves, and all-around brigands for hire. The police were now scouring the hangouts of these men seeking information on where they lived and spent their ill-gotten gains and with whom.

The two transporters were shot to death, they were not robbed since each had over twenty dollars on them and there was no sign of a struggle. They had been kneeling when shot in the back of the head. Holmes views the bodies and the surrounding area nearby and indicates his agreement with the Captain of how the men were executed.

Holmes tells the Captain, "There had to be at least three others here since both men had been shot simultaneously."

"How do you come to that conclusion, I see nothing that would make me believe there were three people."

"I agree, there are no physical signs of three people, nor even one, but if man number one was shot in the head would not the other have been able to move from his subservient position to one of defense, and therefore not fallen in the same way as the first. Plus the head of the tall man fell upon the shoe of the third man who faced them, you can see what remains of his footprint under the head of the tall man. Therefore, there must have been at least three present, one behind each kneeling man and one in front of them and at some prearranged signal the shooter's fire at the same time killing each man."

The Captain was silent for a moment and then says, "I see what you are saying and I find nothing to contradict it, your confirmed high reputation is not understated."

Holmes examines the shoreline upon which the bodies lay and finds it to be of loose stone which yields no apparent indications of any footprints, save for the one under the tall dead man's head. The perpetrators must have walked back up the loosely packed stone through some solid ground beneath a brush path to a heavily traveled thoroughfare that was devoid of any useable information. They must have left and arrived in a coach or wagon. Holmes asks if his constables had followed the path for a reasonable distance to ascertain if the wagon wheel mark from yesterday might be found in the path became more susceptible to yielding a print which could point the direction that the conveyance went.

It was obvious, the men were killed so they would not identify their employer, who must have known they were identified and would shortly be arrested, and would give their employer up.

The employer got the information the men had been described to the police from the listening device at the station and would shortly be apprehended.

Based upon the lack of an apparent struggle, it appears the dead men were caught off guard and were told by their assailants to kneel at gunpoint which they did. Then with two different revolvers, the men were shot, one a 44 and the other a 38.

Unbeknownst to the Captain, Holmes had found some tobacco ash in the stable where Mr. Vincent was found, and not coincidentally, found identical ash at the site of the double murder. Holmes has made an extensive and accurate scientific study of cigar, cigarette, and pipe ash during his absence from 221B Baker Street, he continued collecting samples and knowledge while pursued and courting and marrying Irene. The ash he found was peculiar and not one he encountered previously, and he dedicated himself to matching these ashes with some local or imported ash in the United States. No cigars were found on the murdered men, but a flake of a cigar was found in the large man's shirt pocket.

Holmes kept his knowledge of tobacco ash to himself, because upon his arrival on the first day he noticed a man, evidently English by his suit, reading a copy of the Strand magazine, where Watson had his sensational exploits of Holmes published. He was uncertain if the Captain had read any of these and was concerned this knowledge might destroy his disguise as an English investigator.

Holmes, "Now, I will leave you to your important work of apprehending the murderer."

CHAPTER 16

Churchill Downs

11:30

H olmes leaves for Churchill Downs to join Irene for the afternoon's races and see Bohemian Escape race.

2:30

They watch as Bohemian Escape races in the third race of the day, a five furlough event, against non-winners during the current race season.

At the start, Bohemian Escape is in the middle of the field.

Bohemian Escape jumps out to an early lead.

Irene is out of her seat shouting, "Run Escape run."

Despite her encouragement, Escape tires after four furloughs, but somehow finds a second wind and finishes second by a neck.

Irene is giggling like a schoolgirl as many women in attendance are appalled by her outburst.

Sherlock, "My dear, you are wonderful, so full of life, and not like the other women here, you are in a class all by yourself and I love you for it."

She waved her fifty dollar ticket at him, hugged and kissed him, saying, "Now since the race is done, let us catch some murderers."

"Yes, we shall."

Irene's fifty dollar wager on win, place and show pays sixty dollars, and she was so excited, one would think she won the Derby.

She and Sherlock go to the stables to see Bohemian Escape and arrange for stabling for an uncertain length of time.

4:00

As they are leaving the track, the young constable Hammersmith stops them and says, "The Captain wishes to see you at your hotel, if convenient."

Holmes replies, "Do you know what has happened?"

"No sir, I am just to give you the message."

"Thank you, Constable, we are on our way back to the hotel, and will meet the Captain there."

The Constable leaves to call the Captain, and Irene and Sherlock take a carriage back to their hotel.

CHAPTER 17

Another Victim

4:30

As they enter the hotel, Irene is called to the desk for a message, it is from Mr. or rather Professor Kane seeking an appointment this afternoon, she tells Sherlock and he says it might be an opportune time to visit the Professor, she agrees and says, "I will call and arrange a session for this afternoon."

Sherlock says, "That is grand, have an informative meeting."

While they were talking a hotel page asks, "Are you, Mr. Wallace?"

Holmes replies, "Yes, I am."

"Sir, Captain Williams is waiting in the dining room for you."

Sherlock thanks the page, but before heading to the dining room says goodbye to Irene.

The Captain is seated at a table in a secluded part of the dining room.

Captain says, "There are two matters, first we found the listening post and a dead man, obviously the listener, Willie Peters, a small-time criminal, who previously worked for the telephone company. He was shot in the back of the head like the two thugs this morning. There was paper there, but anything written was probably taken by the killer. The listening device has been removed. Peters was in an infrequently used storage room in this very hotel. The access to that room could be made using a seldom-used back staircase without being observed by anyone. My constables have checked with the entire staff and no witnesses."

Holmes exclaims, "How did they find out we were on the trail of the listener?"

"Perhaps they became suspicious when you ran the bath and did not talk. It is only a guess."

"That might be, what is the second matter?" Holmes thinks I did not tell him of the water ploy?

"It seems to be the thing to kill prostitutes, another was found across the river in Indiana with her throat cut."

Holmes exclaims, " What, why did you not tell that me at once. I need to see the bodies of the prostitutes right now!"

"Why the hurry, they are dead and not going anywhere?"

"There will be more if I am correct."

5:30
Holmes goes across the river, examines the newest body, returns to Louisville, and examines the other body.

CHAPTER 18

Irene's Session with Kane

4:45

Meanwhile, Irene takes a carriage to Mr. Kane's residence in the prestigious Ormsby and Broadway neighborhood.

She pulls the bell cord and the door is opened by Mr. Kane, who says, "Welcome Mrs. Wallace, I am Professor Lucas Kane, and I am most pleased to meet you. Let me say how much I enjoyed your performance at the Gala."

"I am pleased to meet you, thank you for your kind words. Mrs. Ambrose speaks highly of you."

"Yes, Gloria, I mean Mrs. Ambrose is very kind since I feel that I have done very little to help her. But, let us go to the library, and see what may be done to assuage your anxieties."

The library is walled floor to ceiling with books and while Kane closes the curtains to dim the room, Irene sees many books on the occult, spiritualism, and other similar topics.

Kane directs her to a cushioned chair with a small table separating it from another similar chair into which Kane reclines himself.

He asks, "What is bothering you?"

"No matter how brave I may act, I am profoundly bothered by finding the dead Mr. Vincent and even more bothered by the death of the young prostitute."

"Yes, yes, these things are stressful, but maybe I can help."

Continuing he says, "Have you ever had similar feelings?"

"Yes, when my first husband died after a prolonged illness."

"I understand."

He asks for her hand and as he reads her palm.

"I see deep sorrow there and your aura is very conflicted."

Looking into her eyes, "You must put these tragedies out of your mind and meditate twice a day with my meditation writings, which aid the mind and refresh the soul. During your meditations, it is helpful to use some laudanum. I have some for your use, you may take it now to help you."

"I would prefer to take it back to my suite."

"Of course whatever you wish, but remember to use it when you meditate."

5:15

With that the session ends, Kane gives her a copy of his meditations but will accept no payment since she was referred by Mrs. Ambrose, and if Irene needs more help, he will be most happy to assist, with that she bids him farewell and heads back to the hotel.

Holmes' Observations

5:30

While Irene is busy with Kane, Holmes had viewed the corpses and finds each of the dead women have similar cuts to their throats, yet subtly different, although the cuts were made with peculiar knives, the depths of the cuts varied as if done by different persons. Evelyn's cut was deep while the cuts to the other woman were first a shallow cut, followed by a deeper cut to finish the horrible task.

In addition to the cuts, each prostitute had bruising on their wrists and ankles. The bruises were more pronounced on one side of the wrist and ankle, indicating that the women were hanging face down from a higher elevation.

After concluding his examination he returns to the Captain.

6:00

Holmes says, " Captain, I have a strong feeling that the death of the prostitute, Evelyn, has ."

The Captain interrupts, "Evelyn! How in the blazes do you know her name?"

"I was told it at the gala by Mr. Nichols, as was my wife. Is it not public knowledge?"

"No, it is not, we did not find out her name until this morning, after a prolonged interview with her, shall we say, employer, a Ma Fisher. She provides each of her girls with a lockbox within which the girls can keep their personal information. The employer doesn't have a key so that each of the women has some privacy. We only opened Kitten's strongbox this morning and found out her name and where she was from. I have sent an officer out to inform her family, but how on earth did Nichols know her real name when the girls only use a made-up name, and her's was Kitten."

"It seems, he was well acquainted with the girl and she must have confided in him or he with someone else."

The death of the three apparent criminals bother Holmes, but not as much as the death of these two young prostitutes, and their manner of death which was similar to the method by which Jack the Ripper slew his victims in London.

How these deaths tie into the death of Mr. Vincent, was still beyond his grasp.

The Captain responds, "We will find out in a hurry, I will have Nichols brought in, immediately."

"Let us not be hasty. Pulling him in may put the wind up to others, if they learn of our interest in him. Why not watch him and see what he does."

"I will do that."

7:00
The Nichols residence is watched, but no sign of him.

Captain calls Holmes on the telephone, "As a ruse, I sent a fake confidential telegram to Nichols. After the butler did not accept the telegram. I sent officers to his home and questioned the house staff, they said he has not been in since Tuesday and they had not heard from him. The officers received the butler's permission to search the house and found it as the staff had told them. They told the staff to inform the police if Mr. Nichols returns. They said they would since they are quite concerned.

He continues, "I am afraid that Mr. Nichols may have met with an untimely death."

Holmes replies, "Yes, it may be so, but possibly he is hiding in one of the brothels he frequented."

"You may be on to something there, I'll have my officers search every brothel where he might be hiding from top to bottom. If he is in one of them, we will find him."

While the Captain and his forces search for Nichols, Holmes instead of returning to the hotel goes to Nichols' residence, once there, he introduces himself as a private agent helping the police and asks the butler if Mr. Nichols had any frequent visitors.

The butler says, "Yes sir, his most frequent guests have been the General, his valet, the police Captain, Mr. Wilson, and the Colonel."

Holmes thanks him, leaves, and returns to the hotel.

Irene returns to the hotel and dresses for dinner.

CHAPTER 20

Search Vincent's Residence

May 11

7:30

I rene is dressed for dinner, as is Sherlock, but he hesitates going and says to Irene, "My dear will you be able to wait a little longer for dinner since I feel the need to visit Vincent's home."

She says, "I will wait, but I am going with you."

"Of course," he says.

Holmes telephones the Captain, "How is the search for Nichols progressing?"

"We haven't found him yet, but we will."

"I know you will. I have another question, have you searched Vincent's rooms?"

"Yes, my men did a detailed search without finding anything incriminating. But we were not the first ones to search his residence, because it was literally torn apart by person's unknown."

"Would you mind if I took a look?"

"No, of course not. There is a constable there, I will send a note to him permitting you access, and may you have a grand time of it. I hope your search is successful."

"Thank you, Captain, I will try not to be as destructive as the first searchers."

While they get ready to depart, Irene relates her encounter with the mysterious Mr. Kane."

Irene says, "He is a charming charlatan, reading my palm, looking into my eyes seeing that I have a conflicted aura, and tells me to meditate and take laudanum while doing so. As you said, he preys on the weak and lost. I find it amusing in a dark way, now that you are off cocaine, he wants to make me an opium addict."

He says, "Laudanum use to soothe you and get you addicted and reliant on him and his destructive method of control. Mrs. Ambrose must be one of his frequent patients, so sad."

"Yes it is and let us get started on the search of Vincent's residence. The sooner it is over, the sooner we dine."

Sherlock knows there is little danger since the perpetrators have already had their hands on the residence.

8:00
The constable has the note granting them access to the residence. They enter and are amazed how thoroughly the home had been torn apart during the searches it looked like it had been hit by a hurricane.

Sherlock and Irene find the books in the library have been tossed all over. It appears all the books had been rifled to see if they contained letters or notes. Irene and Sherlock rifle every book again, to no avail.

Sherlock is drawn to the bedroom where a large family Bible rests on a dresser top. It has been moved, but not tampered with. Upon examination, the book is quite large and has a latch to hold it together. The latch was quite easy to open and the first page notes it as being the bible of the Vincent family, and an examination of the book discloses no letters, notes, or other information. Sherlock returns the book to the dresser top and looks for other hiding places.

While Sherlock is looking through drawers, under the bed, knocking on the walls for hidden compartments, Irene notices a slight irregularity in the leather binding of the bible, a minor bulge that extended down the entire binding. She shows it to Sherlock and he reacts excitedly and reopening the book, and bending the spine outward he spies a tube in the binding. He uses his pocket knife to remove the tube and inside the tube is a key with W1013 and "LPW" engraved on it, also enclosed is a slip of paper with the name Joseph Smith, evidently the name of the keyholder, likely a pseudonym of Mr. Vincent.

She asks, "Where is the lock that the key unlocks?"

"It is not a bank key, but a key for a secure location where items may be stored. Near our hotel on Main Street is a warehouse, the Louisville Public Warehouse, that has to be it LPW."

"I believe you are right, I have seen it on our carriage rides."

"You are not only beautiful, but ever so observant, I was dismayed, but now I am elated at your find."

"Thank you, my love, but I owe Mr. Poe for the discovery because in his Purloined Letter it was hidden in plain sight, as was this bible and its binding. What do we do next?"

"In the morning, we will go to the warehouse and see what secrets it holds."

"Shouldn't we tell the Captain about our discovery?"

"All in due course, we need to look first."

Irene laughing says, "The game is afoot!"

He laughs, "Very nicely put."

9:00
They return to the hotel for a late supper and evening's rest for tomorrow may be an enlightening day.

CHAPTER 21

The Warehouse

May 12

8:00 AM

After a good night's rest, they have an early breakfast and leave the hotel by nine o'clock.

Sherlock concerned they may be followed has the doorman hail a cab for them.

Once inside Sherlock says to the driver, "Just follow my directions, we may be followed by a disgruntled suitor of my wife, and I want to make certain we are not."

The cab driver replies, "I can do that, sir."

Off they go and take about fifteen minutes before Sherlock feels they are safe, and then tells the driver to take them to the Louisville Public Warehouse.

Arriving at the warehouse, Sherlock thanks the driver and pays him adding a generous tip.

The driver says, "Thank you very much, sir."

The warehouse is a large building situated on Main Street and the river, they enter and are greeted by a stout man behind a desk, who asks, "Good morning, Madam and Sir, how may I help you?"

Sherlock replies, "We need to enter our storage facility."

"Of course, what storage room is it?"

"1013."

"May I see the key and what is your name?"

"Joseph Smith."

"Ay yes", replies to the man and asks Sherlock to sign in, which he does.

Sherlock hands him the key, he looks at it and hands it back saying, "You go through the door on my left, your right."

Irene, "Thank you very much."

The man, a little flustered, says, "You are very welcome."

Once through the door, they are greeted by a very long corridor with numbered doors, and after several minutes arrive at 1013.

Sherlock inserts the key, unlocks the door and they enter a room full of furniture and boxes.

Irene jokingly says, "This should be an easy task."

Sherlock replies, "Quite frankly, I did not believe that Vincent would leave whatever needed hiding in an obvious place, but let us concentrate on the furniture and if we find nothing move onto the boxes."

Irene, "What should I be looking for when I examine a piece of furniture?"

"A piece that appears to have been moved, opened or large enough to be a hiding place."

They proceed to move about the room, Irene to the left, Sherlock the right, and after a time they meet at the back of the room having found nothing, but there is a large wardrobe left to examine. The dust on it is slight, not like the other pieces of furniture.

Irene opens it and sees, shelves, two sets of drawers, and clothes hanging rod. She removes the drawers while Sherlock inspects each shelf and the rod, finding nothing.

Irene starts to replace the drawers, but cannot replace one because it is too deep, so she picks up a less deep drawer and puts in.

Seeing this, Sherlock says, "The drawers are of two different depths, possibly there is a hiding place behind the shallow drawers."

He removes the one Irene has replaced, and he sees a paneled back wall and sees a notch in the upper corner of the back wall, and slight scratch marks on the sidewall. He puts a finger into the notch and pulling, the back wall comes loose and reveals a small shallow iron safe which fills the whole back wall area.

He says, "You have done it again, here is the hiding place of Mr. Vincent's secrets."

She laughs saying, "Of course I found it, I am so very good at sleuthing."

Sherlock examines the safe and says, "It is an old safe and reliable enough to keep things secure from an incompetent cracksman, but not from an expert."

Irene says, "Where will you find this, what is it, a cracksman?"

He says, "You are addressing one."

She exclaims, "What, you can open this safe?"

"Of course, to be as good as I am in what I do, I must know how the criminal does his work. I have studied safe opening and other useful trades."

She says, "Are you certain that you are not descended from brigands and highwaymen?"

"No, I am a country gentleman with unique interests and talents."

"Well, will you please hurry up and open the safe, I am dying of curiosity?"

Bending down in front of the safe, he says, "I am a little rusty, so bear with me."

After two unsuccessful attempts, the third is the charm and he opens the safe and makes a mental note to remember the combination.

He withdraws the contents which include numerous documents in the name of Vincent, letters, deeds, ownership papers for properties, cash, securities, and a single envelope entitled *"Open after my death"*.

Although they want to open the envelope immediately, they do not.

Sherlock says, "We need to find a way to remove this information without carrying the papers in our hands."

Irene points to an old travel bag and says, "This should do it."

"Yes, my dear, it will do very well."

They load the travel bag with the papers, lock the safe, replace the back wall, slide the drawers in, and close the wardrobe.

With that accomplished, they leave the warehouse saying goodbye to the attendant.

CHAPTER 22

Vincent's Secrets

T hey cross the street and enter a small hotel.

They enter the hotel, and say, "We need a small meeting room for the afternoon where we can be private and have a bit of lunch."

The hotel accommodates them, they order lunch, it arrives, they partake rather quickly, and now assured of no more interruptions, they open the travel bag and start examining the contents.

There are several thousand dollars, the deed to his house, securities of local companies, personal letters of his and others, and the *"Open after my death"* envelope.

Once everything is in place, they open the envelope and read the contents side-by-side, the document was written in elegant and extremely legible penmanship as follows:

Satanic Worship and Blood Ritual

A cult resides in the Louisville area that believes in the ritual murder of prostitutes and bloodletting of these women. Through elaborate and secret meetings, the cult members believe by committing these horrific acts they will be endowed by their all-powerful and satanic deity, Lucifer, with long life, power, and untold riches. All members of the cult must take part in the sacrificing of these lost women and when the prerequisite number is thus sacrificed, and the members consume the co-mingled blood of all the victims will they be rewarded with the aforementioned bounties promised by Lucifer.

The prerequisite number to be achieved is eighteen. Now there have been fifteen slain with five in the Northeastern United States, six on the European continent, four in England, and three are needed here to arrive at eighteen. The total is three sets of six or the beast's number of 666.

HOLMES & ADLER AFTER THE FALLS A DEATH AT THE DERBY

I do not know the names of all the cult members, but I know one and it is Andrew Nichols, who related all this to me while in a drug and alcohol-induced stupor while at a brothel. He is enamored with a young prostitute named Kitten. He also said the other cult members had traveled to the continent and the New York City area, but he was reluctant to name any other members. But he alluded to a spiritualist and his paramour. Finally, he said the police at a high level are corrupt, and then he passed out.

I plan to make this cult a very enterprising hobby. I assume from Andrew Nichols's slurred narrative the other members are well to do, and if I apply the right pressure I may become well to do, also.

I do not want to appear to be morbid, but if you are reading this I probably am no longer alive.

If you believe in justice you will run these devils to the ground and have them join me.

Albert Vincent
April 30, 1893

"Mr. Vincent wrote this only twelve days ago, and his blackmail attempt led to his summary execution ten days later."

Sherlock, " I thought there was something sinister in these killings, but nothing like this."

Irene, " I cannot believe it. Lucifer, cults, ritual murder, bloodletting and whatever else, it is beyond my comprehension. May God have mercy on us all, if this is true."

"The murder part is true, the rest is nonsense like so many other cults throughout history, but real or not the killings are brutal and there is warped rational thinking in the whole scheme. From time immemorial, there have been numerous murderous cults killing their own members, slaves, or enemies to placate their gods."

Irene says, " He had the count at fifteen, but it is now seventeen, with the killing of Evelyn and the prostitute in Indiana, with one more to go, to make eighteen. It could be going on right now, and we do not know where to start."

"We must be calm. They need one more prostitute, we must find out if any of the enterprising women in the brothels have had any unusual requests, women making secret off-premises liaisons, having more money, buying more clothing or jewelry. Just maybe we can narrow the search to a few enterprising women. Nichols did not act alone, as Vincent has told us. There are others and I have my strong suspicion that some of the others are part of our list. We know two, Kane and Mrs. Ambrose. I need to find a stationer."

"Why?"

"I need to forge a new letter in Vincent's handwriting with no mention of the spiritualist or paramour nor corrupt police. To do that I need to purchase a suitable pen and ink, a blotter, paper with the same watermark as the original, and a portfolio for mailing."

Irene smiling says, "First I learn you are a safecracker and now a forger, is there no limit to your nefarious skills?

"To defeat crime, one must think and act like a criminal. Now I am off."

To entertain herself, Irene goes through the assorted letters and other documents.

When Sherlock returns, and before he starts his forgery, she says, "My dear, the other letters, he had were for blackmail purposes. He was a devious and cruel man to exploit funds from mostly good people."

"I assumed that when I saw all the letters and the cash, but right now I must do the new letter."

For the next twenty minutes, Holmes writes carefully a new letter from Vincent excluding the comments about police corruption and the two cultists.

He blots the letter, re-read it, has Irene do the same, and once satisfied folds it and puts in an envelope, seals it and writes *"Open after my death"* on the front.

He says, "We have done all that we may accomplish, we must return everything, except the damning blackmail letters or documents, to the safe."

"Why?"

"The Captain needs to find the letter, cash and whatever, except the blackmail correspondence. We will put the blackmail proof in the portfolio, and mail it to ourselves in New Jersey. After doing that, we will go and see the Captain and present him with the key, and beg his forgiveness for being overly anxious to see what was in the warehouse telling him it looked like a big task, so we are now confessing."

"How generous of us. Well, let us be off."

Returning to the warehouse was easy since the stout man had been replaced by a thin man who hardly looked at them as they showed the key and signed. They went to the room, opened the door, the wardrobe and the safe putting the information in the safe and lock it and leave.

CHAPTER 23

Confession

S topping for a coffee, tea, and biscuits, Irene says, "A fine morning's work, and now we look up the Captain."

"Yes, that is the plan."

They hail a cab and ride to the police station in silence.

Exiting the cab, they proceed to enter the station and are greeted by the desk constable, who inquires, "What may I do for you?"

"We would like to see, Captain Williams, please tell him Mr. and Mrs. Wallace are here."

"Of course, I will tell him, and calls the Captain on the telephone." He tells the Captain and says, "He will be right out."

"Thank you."

Moments later, the Captain arrives saying "Good afternoon, please follow me."

They follow him to a meeting room which has unoccupied rooms on each side.

Holmes asks, "Is it safe to speak in here?"

The Captain answers, "Yes."

"In that case, we, I, have a confession to make about Vincent's residence. We found a key hidden in the spine of his family bible, imprinted with the letters LPW, and a slip of paper with the name Joseph Smith and 1013."

"What!"

"Please let me continue, we were so excited, that early this morning we went to the Louisville Public Warehouse and used the key to enter Vincent's storage area. We searched it, but found nothing worthwhile. We decided to let the local experts search the place, and we are truly sorry."

"As you should be. Give me the key, and I will get a detail of men to search the premises. Is there a lot of items?"

Irene responds, "Yes, there is, more than we could do a good job of it."

"My men and I will be going there, and since you have been there you might be some help, so come along."

They all leave the station, and on the way out Irene whispers to Sherlock, "Are we going to be recognized by the man behind the desk?"

"We might be, we need to be lucky."

The Captain leads his men, Holmes and Irene into the warehouse and hands the desk man the key saying, "We need to examine this storage room."

The man behind the desk responds, "That is alright go ahead."

Looking at Irene and Holmes he says, "Back so soon?" Luckily it is the stout man from the morning.

Holmes says, "Yes, but we needed help, thank you." Irene gives the man a radiant smile and the man gets flustered, again.

Captain to Holmes, "Lead the way."

Holmes takes them to the room and the Captain opens the door, and exclaims, "What a lot of furnishings and boxes to look through."

Turning to his men gives orders where to start and what to look for. He is interested in hidden compartments, where evidence may be hidden.

The search begins, Irene finds a suitable chair to sit in, brushing off the dust and Sherlock stands behind her watching with interest the search made by the police.

They examine the wardrobe but find nothing.

Irene rises from her chair and casually walks around the room, looking at this and that. She finally settles in front of the wardrobe and says to Holmes, "We need one of these back home. It is an awfully large piece, but looks good for storage."

The Captain looks over and sees Irene remove a drawer on each side and says, "One side has deeper drawers, but the other does not. Not a good piece of furniture."

She begins to replace the drawers when the Captain steps over and says to Irene, "May I look at the drawers?"

She says, "Of course." and steps out of the way.

The Captain pulls out each drawer and says, "By God, there must be something behind the shallower drawers."

Peering in, he sees the notch, and pulling the back wall away, reveals the hidden safe, and says to Irene, "Madam, you have bested all these men and shown us Vincent's secret place."

He looks at the safe and says, "We cannot open it. Have Fred, the locksmith, hurry over here to open this safe."

An officer scurries out of the room to fetch Fred.

Fifteen minutes go by and the Captain is in an agitated state and at last Fred arrives with his bag of tools.

Fred, "Aye, Captain, what is it you want to be done?"

"Do you think I called you for a sociable drink? I want this safe opened, now, get to it."

"It has a combination lock, these can be mighty tricky, but I will do my best."

"Just open it and be quick about it."

Fred sets to work and after twelve tries and twenty minutes, he opens the safe.

The Captain pushes him aside and standing in front of the safe gathers the contents up and puts them quickly into the same travel bag Irene and Holmes had used earlier. He has Fred give him the combination, as he locks the safe.

Without a thank you to Fred, the Captain says to Holmes, "I am taking this back to the station and I will call you later to come over and see it, goodbye. Here is the key, lock up."

As he is leaving, he tells the lead police officer to have the men put the room in order, which they do in short order and they leave Irene and Sherlock in the room."

She says, "That went as planned."

"Yes, it did. I wonder what the Captain will withhold from us. Onto the hotel and some rest."

Mycroft

May 12

12:00

S herlock did not waste any time at the hotel.

He writes a detailed coded request to Mycroft inquiring about murders of prostitutes similar to the Ripper's on the continent and other parts of England, Ireland, Wales or Scotland, and time was of the essence since lives depend on it.

Also, I need to know if the following people from Louisville, Kentucky - Dr, Richard Jones, Mrs. Vivian Singleton, Mrs. Gloria Ambrose, Miss Natalie Carson, Mrs. Veronica Atkinson, Colonel John Hawthorne, Mr. Charles Wilson, Mr. Andrew Nichols, General Wilbert Wellington, Mr. Gilbert Thompson, Mr. Lucas Kane, and Police Captain Harvey Williams were in England between August and November 1888, the period of the Ripper's atrocities.

Check and see if these same people were on the continent at the same time as the murders found on the continent.

I need the address of a Pinkerton agency near Louisville.

Lastly is there a secure telegraph office where I might be able to send a telegram that is not coded but secure? "

As he writes he lets Irene read the telegram.

Once completed, he rushes to the telegraph office and watches and listens as the message is sent.

He tells the operator to give him the reply as soon as it comes in, anytime it comes in.

Returning to the room, he kisses his wife and suggests a peaceful though thoughtful afternoon and evening as they await the requested information.

He now knows why Vincent was killed, why Evelyn and the Indiana girl were murdered, knows why Nichols must be found. If the cult knows what he has done, he is probably dead because he could not hold his tongue and mourned the killing of Evelyn.

Tobacco

1:00

As he plays his violin, he says, "My dear, I think we should look into the tobacco evidence."

"That is fine idea and a good time to do it while we wait."

Leaving the room they inquire at the hotel reception desk where they may find an excellent tobacconist. They are told the best one in the city is Harold's one block from the hotel.

Thanking him, they head to a quaint bistro with a French ambiance and sit at a secluded table away from attentive ears, order a light lunch with coffee, tea, and biscuits, and discuss the recent events of what is truly an insane enterprise.

Sherlock says, "This cult has a high degree of sanity relative to blackmail by one of all the other cult members."

2:30

Finished with their lunch, they go to the tobacconist shop, hoping he might be able to identify the ash, and if so for whom the compound was made.

Entering the shop they are greeted by none other than the proprietor of the establishment, Mr. Winslow Harold, an extremely tall gaunt man with a handle-bar mustache and stained fingers, undoubtedly from using his own products.

Mr. Harold says, "Good afternoon sir and madam, how may I help you?"

Holmes replies, " Good afternoon, sir. I have a question, have you ever produced a unique tobacco product of Egyptian tobacco with a hint of citrus, bourbon, and cinnamon? "

"Why yes, I have. It is rather unusual."

"Yes, it is a favorite of mine, but I have run out and would like to place an order for a box of them."

"Yes, of course, I would be most happy to prepare a box of them for delivery to you tomorrow at your address."

"We are staying at the Galt House and would like them as soon as possible. Are there others here in Louisville who order this blend from you?"

"Yes, yes. General Wellington, Dr, Richard Jones, and Colonel Hawthorne are repeat customers for this blend."

"That is a very elite clientele for this product. I look forward to the delivery tomorrow."

Holmes pays for the product, and he and Irene leave the shop.

3:00

Irene says, "Well, that was most productive. The three customers for the tobacco are on our list and are also people who knew both Vincent and our Mr. Nichols."

"What a day, my love, what a day! Now let us return to the hotel and await the call from the Captain and what he has learned from Vincent's documents."

Although elated at the findings from the tobacconist, Sherlock is in an agitated state as he awaits word from Mycroft on his telegram request and the Captain on the contents of the safe.

To ease his agitation, Irene asks. "How long do you think we should keep Bohemian Escape here if a week or more I might be able to have him race again if there is a scratch from an upcoming race?"

"What! Of course, that might not be a bad idea, I doubt our next visit to the track will be as momentous, as our first."

"I certainly hope not. What do you think of Kentucky? I find it to be a peaceful and serene area of the country, except for the murders of course. I bought a book in the hotel about Kentucky and read where the area around Lexington is an excellent place to raise racing stock because the water used for the horses is full of pure limestone from deep wells. These limestone deposits in the water are what makes the bones of the horses stronger."

"That is very interesting."

"Yes, when this case closes, let us take a trip to Lexington, it is less then a hundred miles from here."

"Yes, that sounds like a good end to this unexpected mystery."

Captain's Revelations

4:00

A t that moment, the phone rings, it is the Captain who says, "Please come over so we may review the Vincent documents."

Holmes replies, "We shall be right over, Thank you."

Arriving at the station, they are escorted to the Captain who is situated in a small meeting room that is isolated from other rooms.

The Captain says, "We may speak freely here. I have gone through all of Vincent's paper and found only one thing of interest which was an envelope with a statement on it saying "*Open after my death*".

He hands the letter over to Holmes. He and Irene read the forged letter together.

Holmes, "It is incredible, a blood cult, killing prostitutes for human sacrifice and their blood, but it explains why there was so little blood where the bodies were found, they collected the blood. Beyond belief, that this is happening."

Irene, "Vincent noted fifteen killings, but there are now seventeen. My God, they need one more to have eighteen. They must be looking now or have already done the deed."

Captain, "We have no reports of another murdered prostitute, but we must hurry if we are going to stop them."

Holmes agrees and rising to leave with Irene, the door is opened by an officer who says in a decidedly excited manner, "We have Nichols hold up in his favorite brothel and he has said, 'If I go with you I am a dead man'."

The Captain says, "Good news, get more officers and let us leave immediately, come along Mr. Wallace, but Ma'am, I think it would be best if you went back to your hotel."

Holmes, "My dear, I am sorry." Kisses her and hurries from the room with the Captain.

Irene reluctantly agrees and a young officer escorts her out and hails a cab for her.

CHAPTER 27

Nichols

May 12

5:00

A rriving at the brothel, the Captain and Holmes climb the stairs to the top floor of the building and find the constables guarding the door, and they inform the Captain there are men stationed on the street watching the room's window to keep Nichols from exiting.

The Captain addresses Nichols through the door, "Andrew, please let us in and give yourself up, and we will protect you from whatever you fear."

His response is to laugh insanely.

And then Nichols says, "Protect me, you won't protect me, you are as insane as the rest!"

Shouting, "They will kill me mark my words, no one can protect me especially you, nor can your god, if I had a gun I would end it now, do you hear me, I would end it now."

At that, the Captain orders his men to rip the door from its hinges and take Nichols, prisoner. The necessary tools are procured and the destruction of the door is done, the furniture barricading the door is hastily removed and they find Nichols sitting in a corner of the room, wild-eyed and whimpering like a beaten dog.

He says over and over, "I am dead and I going to hell for eternity."

Looking wildly at the Captain he cries, "And you will join me in hell!"

Once inside the room, the Captain tells his men to be gentle because Nichols is hysterical. The officers lift him to his feet and put shackles on his wrists, and start to leave the room.

When Holmes enters he asks Nichols, "Whom are you so afraid of?"

Nichols begins to laugh and says, "The Satanists! The followers of Lucifer. They are everywhere."

The Captain interjects, "That's enough for now Mr. Wallace. We will have time to question him at the station. Let's go men."

Nichols is surrounded by officers with Holmes right behind him as he is maneuvered down the staircase and out onto the porch and down to the street where the police enclosed wagon awaits.

The wagon is positioned forcing Nichols, Holmes, and the police to go around the covered wagon's door. As they move toward the open wagon, a rifle shot is fired and strikes Nichols in the chest and as he falls Holmes stumbles just as a second shot puts a hole in Holmes' bowler hat before striking Nichols in the neck, Nichols falls, and the officers around him crouch behind the wagon dragging the wounded Nichols with them.

Holmes bends down to the wounded man and reaching him, Nichols gasping says with his last breath, "ten deadly sinners, now nine" and dies.

CHAPTER 28

Snipers

5:30

H olmes turns and looks at the buildings across the street and sees a curtain billowing out of an open window and shouts above the din, "Captain, the shooter is across the street in that gray building on the second floor third window on the left"

The Captain yells to his men to go to the front and rear of that building, but it is too late to capture the shooter, when they enter the room Holmes had indicated, they can still smell the burned powder and see a sniper's nest made from old furniture for the rifle rest.

The search of the building finds no other occupants, the building was either abandoned or simply between tenants.

Holmes inquires of the Captain, " Could you have taken Nichols out another way from the brothel?"

"Yes, the rear service entrance, but it would have been much more crowded."

"A search must be made immediately of any building that faces the rear of the brothel for another sniper's nest. Our adversaries would not rely upon one place to attack Nichols."

The Captain orders two officers to search the buildings having a view of the brothels' rear door.

Holmes heads across the street and enters the sniper's nest, and carefully examines the room and finds on the floor, a spent cigar and its ash, he scoops these up and places each in folded paper.

He returns and goes around the brothel and peruses the scene of the second sniper's nest, and enters the building where the police congregate. He proceeds to the room and finds a similar nest and more cigar ash but it was not as recent as the other.

Returning to the brothel, he asks the Captain, "Have you instructed your men to ask any people in the area, who might have seen the shooter and his fellow sniper in either building."

Replying, Captain agitatedly says, "Of course, my men are scouring the neighborhood seeking out anyone who might have seen the assailants."

It is evident to Holmes, his protagonists had time to plan the entire operation, like a military operation, and they knew Nichols whereabouts before the police knew. Holmes ponders, were the assassins fortunate to have found Nichols, or did they get information from inside the brothel? Did they check each brothel looking for him, or offer payment to anyone who would provide the necessary information.

Sometime later, the Captain informs Holmes that his men have found only one person who might have seen something, but he, crazy Levy Franks, is known to the police as one who exaggerates many things to try and garner some good feeling from the police.

Nichols' body is removed from the scene in the police covered wagon.

Holmes says to the Captain, "In the time that Nichols vanished until he came to light in the brothel, what did the police do to try and find him?"

"We went and checked each brothel, inquiring if he was there or if he had been seen there."

" I surmise the occupants were not very forthcoming, or simply said they had not seen him. I believe that the occupants were unlikely to answer any questions from the police. Captain, let us ask the madam, how much she was offered to provide information about Nichols, and who offered it."

The Captain replies, "Well, let's do that right now."

Holmes did not think that this was the time or place to bring the Captain up to date on the ash evidence.

CHAPTER 29

Ma Fisher's

6:30

They enter the brothel, and find the madam, Ma Fisher, in the parlor and the Captain goes directly to the question, "How much were you paid to tell that Nichols was hiding here?"

She says, "I do not know what you are talking about, I was not asked nor paid by anyone, I liked Mr. Nichols and would not have put him in any jeopardy."

Holmes interjects, "Are all of your women as scrupulous as you, or are there some who might for a few dollars disclose his residing here?"

"Yes, there are some who will tell tales if the monies are good. I will get those I suspect of such treachery and let you question them."

"Thank you, mam."

The madam leaves the parlor and after a short while returns with three women, and introduces them to the Captain and Holmes.

The first is Esther a thin red-haired woman of about 25 years with big hard looking eyes.

The second is Rhonda a large woman with black hair small blue eyes which appear to be laughing at the whole scene.

The last is Crystal, a petite brunette with eyes darting between the Captain, Holmes, and Ma Fisher.

The Captain says, "Ladies, we have only one question for you.."

Before he continues, Holmes interrupts him and looking at

Rhonda, says "Those are remarkable earrings you have. My wife has a similar pair, but not as brilliant as those. When did you receive them?"

For a large woman, she appears to shrink before their eyes, and shakily says, "I have had these for a long time, sir."

Esther interjects saying, " You just got those, I know because I have been through your stuff, they were not there yesterday, and I have never seen you wear them before,"

Crystal confirms it saying. " Aye, you never wore those until today."

Holmes says "What man gave them to you and for what?

She quietly says, " He enjoyed my services, that's all, and that's the god's ..."

The Captain walks towards her, interrupts barking says, "Keep god out of this, you are lying, who was the man, was he a regular client or a stranger looking for information?"

She begins to shake, tears well in her eyes, and sputtering says, "I never saw him before, but he asked if I could help him find Mr. Nichols because Nichols owed him money and wanted to get paid before he was hurt for not paying. He paid me twenty dollars, gave me these here earrings, and I told him. I never thought Mr. Nichols would come to any harm, I swear before God."

The Captain now calm says, "Could you describe him to us, we need to find him."

"He was a weasel of a man like a broke down jockey, he had a right-sided limp, a red mustache and an opium smell."

7:00
The Captain says, "I know him, he is Paulie Newman, a former jockey who fell badly several years back, never could ride again and has been in and out of my jail on numerous occasions for

drunkenness and petty theft. We should be able to find him soon enough. You ladies are dismissed, but do not leave the city, especially you, Rhonda."

When leaving, Rhonda asks, "Am I in trouble with the law?"

Captain, "Not at this time."

After they depart the brothel, Holmes looks at the Captain saying, "I firmly believe the diminutive Mr. Newman will not be found alive. He has served his purpose to the unholy cult and will be sacrificed on their Satanic altar."

Leaving the scene, Holmes returns to the hotel and Irene and a good night's rest. Eager to resume the hunt in the morning.

More Revelations

May 13

8:00

A fter a good night's sleep, Sherlock arises early, and orders breakfast for Irene and himself, and over breakfast, Irene reads the account of Mr. Nichols's murder, and Sherlock certain that they cannot be overheard fills in the newspaper's omissions.

One omission not mentioned to Irene, Sherlock asks, "Irene please come and sit on the divan with me, I have something to tell you."

"Why so serious, my love?"

"The paper relates that two shots were fired, I know the second was intended for me, had I not stumbled trying to hold Nichols, the second bullet would have hit me in the head instead of just going through the top of my hat."

"On my lord, they are trying to kill you."

"It appears so, my helping the police has made some progress and the cult has had enough of me. The second bullet would have been written off as a bad shot by the assassin, and not an attempt on my life."

"What are you going to do?"

"Keep on the case, but we must be vigilant. I am so sorry that you should have to go through this."

"Sherlock, my love, I knew what you have done for a career and the dangers you must sometimes endure, and I will endure them by your side."

While seated, Sherlock continues, "When we reviewed the letter and the contents of Vincent's safe with the Captain, I did not see any of the cash Vincent kept in the safe. I believe that the Captain kept it for himself. Vincent was writing the truth when he wrote that the upper members of the police are corrupt."

"Nor did I notice any cash, so our nice Captain is not so honest."

They dress for another day in the city wondering what the day will hold for them. They exit their suite and leave the hotel asking the doorman to hail a cab for them.

A carriage arrives and they head to the police station to find out what has transpired while he rested.

108

CHAPTER 31

The Snitch

10:00

Once there, Holmes and Irene meet with the Captain in his office.

The Captain starts with, "Mrs. Wallace, what I am going to relate is not a subject for a lady, it is gruesome."

Irene responds, "No more gruesome than the seven people murdered recently. So please continue."

The Captain says, "Yes ma'am, Well, it is now eight."

Holmes interjects, "When did they find the late Mr. Newman and how was he dispatched?"

"Well, sir, as you said last night he did not survive the evening. His body was found in an alley next to a saloon, he frequented regularly. His throat was cut, and he was left there to bleed out. It was a nasty bit of work, not a very clean job, at all."

Holmes, "So our murderers leave no loose ends, once they get what they want they remove any links to themselves."

"Aye", says the Captain, "they never even attempted to make it look like a robbery because he had thirty dollars in his pocket. We searched his body and found nothing of interest. We searched his room and it was barely furnished. No leads there that we could find. Another blank wall."

Holmes asks, "I need to find a secure telegraph office where I may send a message concerning the Crown as I believe a reply to my last message has been lost. It is of the utmost urgency."

"The best place for security is the Fort Knox telegraph office. The Fort is thirty-five miles from here. I know the fort commander, Colonel Waterson, I will call him right now and request that you have secure access to his telegraph."

The Captain places a telephone call to the Fort and is connected to Colonel Waterson and the Captain proceeds to make the request, and after several minutes of questioning, agrees to permit Wallace to use the telegraph.

He hands the telephone to Holmes, who thanks the Colonel for permitting him to use the fort's telegraph.

The call ended, Irene and Sherlock say farewell to the Captain and leave.

CHAPTER 32

Fort Knox

2:30 PM

I rene and Sherlock catch a cab and head to the nearest telephone exchange. Upon arrival, they take precautions to keep Sherlock from being overheard, Holmes calls Fort Knox seeking Colonel Waterson.

The fort answers the call and Holmes asks for the Colonel.

He reluctantly answers, "Good afternoon, again, Mr. Wallace, I received the telegram from London requesting that I give you my cooperation in whatever you are doing, and letting you have use of our telegraph. Why did you not know this when you were with the Captain?"

"I was unaware, that you did receive the reply telegram. I never received a reply. I desperately need the use of your telegraph.

Thank you Colonel for granting this unique request, and I will be there as soon as possible today."

"You are welcome. You may not be aware but it is a solid three to four-hour ride to the fort. You will need to change horses about halfway which is West Point. Good luck and I will see you later today. Goodbye."

3:30

Sherlock and Irene hurry to the hotel, Irene is pleased to be included in this adventure, and orders a picnic lunch for their journey. Sherlock arranges for transportation to the Fort with a change of horses halfway as suggested by the Colonel.

CHAPTER 33

Fort Telegraph

3:30

They put the carriage horse to a mighty test, and when they arrive at the halfway station in West Point, Kentucky, the tired horse is replaced with a fresh one.

While they wait, they eat their picnic lunch, and once refreshed the new horse is hitched, they immediately leave for the fort.

6:30

Arriving at the fort, Holmes and Irene are greeted by the fort's commander Colonel Emerson Waterson, a ramrod erect officer with a well-trimmed mustache, and the physique of a career trained military man.

He says, "I expected you sooner based upon the telegram we received from London which we replied in the affirmative, so I am confused why did the Captain make the same request?"

Holmes unsurprised says, "I never received a return telegram from London, it was not delivered to me. I asked the Captain to request your aid to find out if he would follow through. He did, but I felt it was very reluctantly."

"What you ask is a truly unique request. Do you not trust the telegraphy offices in Louisville or the Captain?"

"Yes sir, I do not. As I hastily told you, I am concerned a return telegram to me has been deliberately withheld from me by parties to a series of murders in Louisville. You may have read about the rash of killings, and as I told you on the telephone I am helping the Captain with his investigation and truly need your help if we are to bring the murderers to justice."

"I understand, I will do whatever I can to help you in your

mission. My orderly will escort you and your wife to our telegraphy office."

4:00

When they arrive at the telegraph station, the orderly informs the telegraph operator of the Colonel's instructions to leave the office to Mr. Wallace and his wife. The operator is to check every hour with Wallace for any messages that have been received for the fort.

Sherlock, after being left with only Irene in the office, re-sends his coded request to Mycroft.

The message sent, he and Irene take as much comfort in the telegraph office as possible awaiting the reply. As they wait, they receive fort related communications which they write up, give to the fort telegrapher each hour for delivery. When needed they send replies.

7:00

Several hours later, the Colonel has dinner brought to them.

Mycroft's Reply

8:00

A fter dinner, a response to his request arrives, and starts with the admonition, "I sent this information previously."

Mycroft's telegram begins. "My inquiries have disclosed the following about similar murders and the whereabouts of your suspects.

In 1888, in France three prostitutes were murdered by throat-cutting, in 1890, in Italy, three had their throats slit, and four butchered in the same way in London. Ten women killed like the work of the Ripper.

Of your suspect's list, the following were in France, Italy, and London at those times: Mrs. Ambrose, Colonel John Hawthorne, Dr, Richard Jones, Mr. Andrew Nichols, General Wilbert Wellington, Mr. Charles Wilson, Captain Williams, and Lucas Kane.

Mrs. Singelton, Miss Carson, and Mr. Thompson were not in France at those times.

Mrs. Atkinson was not in England at that time.

Your suspect list has been reduced to eight.

Are there more similar murders in the United States?

Concerning a secure telegraph office, the most secure is at Fort Knox, Kentucky about 35 miles from Louisville. I have contacted the fort and its commander, Colonel Waterson, and requested that you be accommodated private use of his telegraph office as a special favor to the British government. You will need to go there and present yourself.

Lastly, there is an unofficial office of Pinkerton in Louisville. Your credentials have been sent to his office in Cincinnati and that office will secretly notify him, you will need to call him for a meeting, just tell the telephone exchange to connect you with Mr. Aloysius Washington."

After decoding the telegram, Sherlock agrees with Mycroft's conclusions about who was where and when. Though not convincing, they were damned by how closely their journeys matched up with the deaths of other prostitutes in the regions, they visited both on the continent and England.

Holmes sends a note of thanks to Mycroft saying he would no longer be receiving telegrams at the fort. Gathering his notes from Mycroft they head back to Louisville, after thanking Colonel Waterson for his help in the matter.

12:00
They make the trip back to the hotel arriving just after twelve.

CHAPTER 35

Obvious Omission

A t the hotel, Sherlock and Irene are getting ready for bed.

Irene says, "I need your help. I am unable to unfasten the back of my dress."

"Certainly, my dear, at least that is a task which I can accomplish since I am not able to solve this case."

"Do not fret, you will as always, solve it, and then you will not have to do such a minor task as unbuttoning my dress, since we will be home, and Alice will do it for me. It is quite surprising how dependent we become on our servants, not servants, really, but members of the household."

"Quite true, after the Falls, I discovered how much I relied on Watson, Mrs. Hudson, and Wiggins, the leader of the irregulars, for many tasks that made life easier."

He pauses, shakes his head and slaps the side of it with his palm and exclaims, "What a fool I have been, what a fool!"

Irene concernedly asks, "What on earth is wrong, my dear?"

"I have fallen into a trap, a trap of following the obvious, and not looking at any other possibilities. All of our suspects are well to do, and of course have many servants, some of whom travel with them. These people are basically invisible to us. They are opening doors, driving carriages, cooking, dressing, cleaning, and any other tasks the lord and lady of the manor do not do."

Irene, "You think one of them could be the killer?"

"It is a possibility."

Public Telephone

May 14

8:00 AM

T he following morning finds Sherlock in good spirits as he breakfasts with Irene in their room, and he peruses the local morning newspaper, the Courier-Journal, looking for any mention of the murders of the various individuals associated with the case. The only mention is that the police are making headway into the murders of Vincent and Nichols, but no mention of progress on the murdered prostitutes and thugs.

10:00 AM

Leaving the hotel, Holmes asks a cab driver to take them sightseeing with a lazy ride meandering through various streets, and finally convinced that they are not be followed asks the driver, "Please take us to the nearest public telephone exchange."

"Yes sir"

10:30

They arrive at a public telephone exchange, pays the driver with a nice tip, and enter the exchange. Sherlock secures an end telephone room and asks, "My dear, will you keep an eye out for any eavesdroppers?"

Irene says with a smile, "I shall maintain security."

"Thank you, dear."

Holmes asks the operator to connect him to Aloysius Washington.

After several rings, a man answers saying, "Hello, how may I help you?"

"Is this Mr. Washington?"

"Yes, the one and only, and who might you be?"

"I am Mr. Reginald Wallace, I believe you received my credentials from a friend in England."

"Aye, the mysterious Mr. Wallace. I got the telegram and I am here to assist you if I am able."

"Is there some secure place where we may meet?"

"Aye, I have quarters above a nice family restaurant, Frankies, that serves an excellent lunch. I would suggest that you come to lunch here and request the private curtained dining room number one. Once in the room, close the curtains and I will enter through the back and we may talk there or upstairs in my residence."

"My wife and I will be over shortly and lunch will be good. See you soon."

The call ends, Sherlock and Irene leave the exchange, hail a cab and head to Frankies.

CHAPTER 37

Pinkerton

12:30

O nce again, they take a circuitous route to shake any followers,

Arriving at Frankie's, they request dining room number one and are escorted there, and the curtains are closed. Almost immediately, a curtain covered door opens at the back of the dining room and Mr. Washington enters asking them to follow him.

They take a flight of stairs up to his residence, and once inside he introduces himself, "I am Aloysius Washington, a Pinkerton Agent, without a true office, but located here to assist in any matters that may come up."

Holmes does the introductions, "I am Reginald Wallace and this is my wife, Irene."

"Pleased to meet you both. I assume you are ready for lunch so I ordered for you and the meals will be up soon."

Irene, "How thoughtful of you, and thank you."

"My pleasure, now onto business, the telegram told me very little."

Holmes says, "Yes, sorry for the mystery, but it is necessary. There have been numerous murders in Louisville all of which are unsolved, and I am in the middle of a heinous plot to kill at least one more. Are you acquainted with Captain Williams of the police force?"

"Yes, I have not had any direct contact with him, but my predecessor in Louisville had several contentious encounters with Williams."

"How so, if you do not mind my asking?

"John, the former unofficial agent here, had run to ground a thief of grand criminal achievements, but when John asked for assistance in apprehending the thief, he was put off. Shortly thereafter the thief disappeared, and John believed that Williams had warned the man plus John thought Williams had been well compensated for the warning and may have even assisted in the man's disappearance. John holds Williams in high contempt."

"What is your opinion of the Captain?"

"Based upon what John said, and my observance of him and stories related to Williams, I find that he is most likely corrupt or severely incompetent, or both. The current situation you mentioned of the unsolved murders is in keeping with his reputation."

Holmes hesitates, but then says, "These murders are all related to a cult of devil worshipers, please read this letter written by the deceased Mr. Vincent."

Holmes hands Washington Vincent's letter and he reads it.

After reading it, Washington says, "This is sadistic, and you say all the murders are part of the work of this cult."

"Bear with me. Vincent was very likely killed because he tried to blackmail members of the cult, based upon information from Andrew Nichols. If I had not been at the track that day, his death would have deemed a heart attack, which was the Captain's original thought, but I showed him proof that it was murder. The men who dropped Vincent in the stall were identified and murdered the next day. Our hotel room was subject to a listening device on the telephone, the listener was found the next day murdered like the thugs who dumped Vincent. Nichols tried to hide from the cult but was trapped in a brothel and quickly assassinated, as was the man who told the cult where he was. In between these murders was the brutal killing of two young prostitutes, whose deaths and blood are needed for the cult's ritual. There you have it. With those killings, they are only short one more sacrifice to complete the ritual."

Washington was slow to respond, and finally says, "Ghastly! What do you want me to do?

"I have a list of persons, whose travels around the United States I need to know if they were in the Northeastern part of the country at the time of similar murders in that region. I believe that Pinkerton is best equipped to gather the information, but I would not rely on the local telegraph office, since I believe they are compromised."

"I have no need of the telegraph for this since I send daily dispatches to the office in Cincinnati, and I would expect a reply the next day. I can express the urgency and follow-up, if needed, with a telegram to a fictitious person in Cincinnati instead of to the Pinkerton office seeking a quick reply."

"Very good, now here are the names of those I need to be investigated, and any servants who travel with them and any other pertinent details, your agency can find out. Mrs. Gloria Ambrose, Colonel John Hawthorne, Dr, Richard Jones, Mr. Andrew Nichols (deceased), General Wilbert Wellington, Mr. Charles Wilson, Captain Harvey Williams, and Mr. or Professor Lucas Kane. I need to know of similar murders in the Northeastern United States, where I believe that five have been killed since we know of ten in England and the continent and two here for a total of seventeen. We need haste to find to stop the killing of number eighteen."

"I understand."

At that moment there is a knock on the door, and rising Washington opens the door to a waiter with lunch for them.

Washington thanks the waiter, and says, "Now let us have lunch, and while doing that I shall write up my dispatch to the office. It will be ready to go, right after we eat."

While eating, Washington writes between bites of lunch.

Holmes asks, "I am curious why an unofficial presence in Louisville, is there a case you are working on? If you cannot reply, I understand."

"I can tell you since you mentioned one of my suspects, Mr. Charles Wilson. I am keeping track of shipments of stolen and smuggled artifacts from the West and the Orient. I have been building a case for several months, and shortly, we will make an arrest, or should I say the U.S. Marshals will make the arrest since as I have said, the local police cannot be relied upon. Wilson is a primary smuggler and it is the basis of his wealth."

"Thank you for that, Wilson indeed, and the lunch was excellent, as you said it would be."

Washington shows Holmes the dispatch, and Holmes agrees that it is accurate.

2:00 PM
Holmes and Irene are led down to the dining room. To maintain the appearance of having lunched in the room, there are used dishes, glasses, and luncheon ware on the table. They pay their bill leave the restaurant and go to the police station.

CHAPTER 38

Tobacco Evidence

2:00

They ride from the restaurant to the police station with only a few comments about the good weather. Arriving shortly after two in the afternoon, they are ushered into the Captain's office by a police sergeant.

Once seated, Holmes says, "Is this room safe from eavesdroppers, both on the premises and outside?"

"Yes, as you know the phone connection has been eliminated, and a guard stands outside of earshot to assure privacy."

"Good, it is what I expected. Do you have a few minutes concerning something I need to quiz you about?"

"A quiz?"

"Yes, my question is what brand of cigar do you smoke?"

"Your question is what brand of cigar do I smoke?"

Holmes sighs and says, "Yes, that is my question and it is quite important."

"I have no particular brand. When I buy cigars, they are not the cheapest, but near the middle in price, as you may not know as a Captain, I do not make enough to buy the best."

"I thought as much, but I had to ask and I am now certain, I can go forward with the topic of cigars."

Exasperated, the Captain says, "What topic of cigars? What on earth are you talking about?"

"Let me start at the beginning. In the stable where Vincent was dropped, I found cigar ash of a unique blend, at the site of the execution of the thugs, I found the same ash, in both of the snipers' nests at the brothel, I found the same ash, at that site you were smoking a cigar the produced the same ash, and again in our suite, you smoked the same."

"What, you suspect me, I will be damned, sir. Excuse me, Ma'am."

Irene, "You are excused."

"I do not suspect you as a killer, but someone who has acquaintance with the killer or killers. Recently, Irene and I visited a local tobacconist shop searching for the particular cigar which would produce that ash, and we found one. He procures this particular blend for three people, and I now know one of them gave you a cigar. I need to know because one of them is a killer, an accomplice, or employs the killer."

"Wait, how do you know so much about cigar ash?"

"I read an interesting monograph on the subject written by a fellow Englishman, Mr. Sherlock Holmes, and found it quite enlightening, and helpful in a few cases, with this one in particular."

"Well, who are these people? I bring them right in and get the information we need from them. I cannot wait to end this murderous case"

"I have no specific case against any one person, but I know that the tobacco in question is purchased locally by three men, Colonel Hawthorne, Dr. Richard Jones, and General Wellington.

"On occasion, each of these three men has been kind enough to give me one of their fine cigars."

"Good, good, that answers my question."

"Tobacco ash is not evidence that these men are involved in these heinous crimes."

Holmes agrees and asks if there are any new developments, and the Captain responds there are none.

The business at hand concluded Sherlock and Irene leave the Captain to his urgent task.

Another Telegram

2:30

U pon entering the cab, Holmes says to the driver, "Take us to the nearest public telephone exchange?"

The driver says, "Yes, there is one about one block from here."

"Yes, take us there and wait for us, if you may."

"Yes, sir."

3:00 8:00 in London

When arriving at the exchange, Sherlock and Irene, enter and find a corner telephone compartment empty.

Sherlock asks, "Irene, my dear, please stand guard outside to make certain no one may overhear my conversation."

Sherlock withdraws a handwritten coded message to be sent to Mycroft, which he had prepared before going to the police station.

Irene stands outside the compartment and watches for anyone who might eavesdrop.

With Irene on guard, Holmes asks the exchange operator to connect him with Colonel Waterson at Fort Knox. After a slight delay, the colonel answers the call."

Holmes starts, "Good afternoon Colonel. I am calling with another request. I need information about some other people, who may or may not be involved in the Louisville murders."

"Good afternoon and how may I help you."

"I would like to once again use your telegraph since it is secured and not public. I would like to have a telegram sent to a contact of mine in England, to do this I will be sending the message in code for extra security, therefore I need to tell your telegraph operator what the message is and have him send it, and when a response is received, call me at the Galt House that the reply has been received, and I will call the Fort from a public telephone exchange and transcribe the message. I know this is strange, but I do not know who is friend or foe."

"Indeed, it is strange, but I will help. I will call in a telegrapher to take down your message and send it immediately."

"I am greatly indebted to you, and with your help, we may be able to end this ghastly enterprise."

Holmes reads the telegram to the telegrapher and has him read it back to him, it is done.

3:30
Returning to the hotel, they decide to rest and have tea, coffee and biscuits brought to their room.

Knowing that it will be a long wait for the information from England, they leave the hotel for a stroll and some shopping, since they have had little time for any such mundane activity.

They return to their suite, Sherlock plays his violin while Irene reads a Stevenson novel, The Strange Case of Dr. Jekyll and Mr. Hyde.

She says, "My dear, you might find this amusing, I am reading this novel for something less gruesome, than our case."

Sherlock tries to relax but paces the floor of their suite awaiting the call from the Colonel, telling them he has received the reply telegram.

6:00
The telephone rings and Holmes answers and hears the fort telegrapher say, "Mr. Wallace, sir, I have your telegram."

"Thank you, that was quick work, I will call you from a public telephone exchange, and you can read it to me."

<u>6:30</u>
Irene and Sherlock, leave the hotel, go to the telephone exchange, calls the fort telegrapher, and he reads the telegram to Holmes.

"Thank you so very much."

The contents of the telegram are quite extensive and detailed.

<u>7:00</u>
Returning to the hotel, Sherlock remarks, "Mycroft and his contacts have outdone themselves with their replies."

He quickly decodes the telegram and reads it to Irene.

"Mrs. Gloria Ambrose, Lady's maid Ruth Thomas, Butler William Eagers 36, and traveling companion Mr. Lucas Kane; Colonel John Hawthorne and Valet Ralph Matthews 31; Ret. General Wilbert Wellington and Valet Jacob Hacker 27 and traveling companion Captain Harvey Williams;   Mr. Charles Wilson and Valet Samuel Henderson 29 and Dr. Richard Jones travels alone."

She asks, " Is it what you wanted?"

"Yes, it is indeed. Now we need the Pinkerton information."

CHAPTER 40

Warning

8:00

I rene says, "I am starving, may we now go to dinner. After which I will amuse myself with Dr. Jekyll and Mr. Hyde, a very nice bedtime story."

"Yes, I am famished, let us find a nearby restaurant for our dinner, and then a good night's sleep."

Unbeknownst, to Irene, Sherlock is carrying his revolver.

10:00

Returning to the hotel from their dinner, Sherlock opens the door to their suite and sees an envelope on the floor, it has no address, but just a single word,

WARNING.

He closes the door, moves to the divan, opens the envelope, inside is a single sheet of paper, based on its watermark, it is from the hotel.

Sherlock reads the message aloud to Irene.

This is your first and last warning, we missed you at the brothel. We will not miss again. If you cherish your wife and your life, leave now and go back to New Jersey while you still can, or prepare to meet your maker.

She says, "You really have upset them."

"Indeed, I think it might be best if you take Bohemian Escape and go back to New Jersey."

"No, that is not to be. I will not leave you. I am needed here with you."

"I will not be able to function properly if I know that you are in danger."

"I am not a delicate little flower, I believe I proved that when I bested you. I will carry my pistol wherever I go, and I am a crack shot. I do not fear these people, they will not sneak up on me and cut my throat. Never fear, you continue until you bring them down."

"Is there nothing, I can say to dissuade you?"

"Nothing at all, now let us get ready for bed. Once rested we will bring the hounds of hell under our heel. Now let us go to bed."

CHAPTER 41

Subterfuge

May 15

8:00

A fter a peaceful night's rest, they breakfast in their room.

While dressing for the day, Irene asks, "What is the next step?"

"I need to find a theatrical makeup store to engage in some subterfuge, and I need to hide my whiskers with a larger more full beard, and purchase necessary materials for this other persona."

"Ay yes, like the old wounded religious man, when we first met."

'Yes, indeed my lad bidding me goodnight at Baker Street as you planned your honeymoon trip to the continent."

9:00

They leave the hotel shortly after nine for the telephone exchange. Holmes telephones Aloysius Washington and is given the addresses of the six potential suspects and their aides, all of whom live in the prestigious Ormsby and Broadway area of the city.

Holmes asks, "Any word?"

"None, but afternoon, probably."

"Thank you."

Sherlock, "Now let us find the shop I need, gather my wardrobe, and locate the abodes of our suspects, after which we will need a good lunch, any place you wish."

Finding a theatrical costume house, Holmes purchases what he needs for his disguise has his bundles taken to the hotel while he and Irene stroll about in the center of the city. Finding a chic little cafe with a European flair they have a quiet meal without a conversation about killings.

After lunch, they take a Louisville Transfer carriage to explore the addresses of the six suspects and their aides. All six have spacious residences in the Ormsby Avenue and Broadway section of Louisville, predominated by large two and three-story homes.

Persona

H olmes considers various approaches to each residence and returns to the hotel to map out his strategy for the next day since if he is correct the eighteenth murder will take place very soon.

The disguise complete, he asks Irene for her assessment.

She says, "You look like an ordinary workman, which is what I assume you want to appear."

"I plan to be a scissor grinder.'

She laughs sadly and says, "How truly ironic portraying one's self as a sharpener of scissors and knives to catch a person who cuts throats with a knife."

"Very ironic, indeed, how perceptive of you, I conceived the idea just for that purpose. I hope to find out what knives each household needs sharpening. So, I looked for a trade that would give me access to the neighborhood without being intrusive."

1:00
He leaves Irene at the hotel in disguise and asks the doorman about any scissor grinders in the area. The man gives him the names and locations of several.

He hails a cab and goes to the establishments mentioned by the doorman and asks each if they, "Do business in the Ormsby and Broadway area of the city?"

He is successful on the third try and then asks, the grinder by the name of Louis on what days of the week does he service that area and the scissor grinder responds, "Tuesday is my normal day for that neighborhood starting at nine o'clock."

"Excellent," replies Holmes and rents the man's horse and equipment for the day and the use of his stable to disguise himself. The vendor was most obliging because of the large sum Holmes paid him.

The grinder instructs Holmes on how to ply his trade, "Just call out, scissors and knives and other things needing sharpening, and pause allowing the help to get out to the street."

Chuckling he says, "If they ask where I am tell 'em, I won big at the races and now have to recover from my winnings."

Holmes is also told to use the pricing chart affixed to the wagon for each task.

With a few lessons, in doing the sharpening tasks he is ready to start his investigation at nine o'clock Tuesday morning.

Returning to the hotel, Holmes is ready to investigate his suspects, but he is telephoned by Washington and told it has arrived.

Holmes says, "We will be right over."

Telling Irene, they make haste to see Washington.

News from Pinkerton

2:00

Entering the dining room one at Frankie's, they are joined by Mr. Washington and taken to his flat. He hands Holmes the dispatch from the Cincinnati Pinkerton's about the six suspects and their servants.

It reads as follows:

"There were five similar killings in the Northeastern United States, and one of your suspects was not in the vicinity of the murders, Dr. Richard Jones, he was out West at the times of the killings.

The following were all in the vicinity of the five killings:

Mrs. Ambrose, a lifelong Louisville native, head of several charities for the poor and orphaned children. She is very wealthy. Lost her sons were lost in the Civil War and her husband died shortly thereafter, some say of a broken heart.

William Eagers, the butler of Mrs. Ambrose, 36, rose from assistant to housekeeper to butler, unmarried, likable man with a strong body, light brown hair, stands nearly six feet tall, has a hawk-like face with dark blue eyes that seem to never let anything go unnoticed.

Colonel John Reginald Hawthorne, 52, from Covington, Kentucky, educated locally, widowed, enlisted in the Union Army, distinguished career advanced to Colonel before end of the war in 1865, severely wounded losing most of the use of his right arm, left service in 1885, back to Kentucky, inherited meat processing plant in Louisville, lawyer, former state legislator, well thought of, very good standing in society, no blemishes on his person.

Colonel's valet Ralph Matthews, 31, from Lancaster, Kentucky, joined the army in 1880, became Colonel Hawthorne's aide, de camp in 1884, has been by his side since, married, two children, resides with wife Lilith in the residence of Colonel, she is house-keeper, he is butler and valet. No unsavory reports about the couple, or their children. Matthews is of medium height, a bit on the heavy side, competent soldier with good military skills.

Mr. Charles Wilson, 31, born in Louisville, wealthy family, an only child, parents killed in a railroad accident, he inherited a fortune, apparently devastated, turned to drink squander-ing most of the family inheritance on a lecherous life, until he met his valet, Samuel Henderson, lay preacher seeking to convert prostitutes and customers, one of whom was Wilson, who fell under Henderson's spell, turned away from wayward life, a small amount of inheritance intact. Since that time, Wil-son started his business as a dealer in art objects of all kinds, increased his wealth, and at the persuasion of Henderson be-came very charitable towards the poor, services to teach poor children to read and write, and began a series of homes where prostitutes could try to earn a better life and get educated. He is currently a suspect in artifact smuggling.

Mr. Samuel Henderson, valet, 29 years, from Paducah, Kentucky, father was minister, two siblings died early on from smallpox or cholera, entered seminary, did not graduate became a zealot of spreading the good news and attacking the sinners with the hope of saving them, the biggest conversion was Wilson, never married since he believes that doing so would diminish his evangelization efforts. Henderson is a diminutive man of about five foot two weighing about one hundred thirty pounds, carries a box with him when he preaches so he may be seen and heard. No unsavory or questionable matters have been dis-covered on either man and they seem to be what they are, caring and god-fearing individuals.

Retired General Wilbert Albert Wellington, 62, from Frankfort, Kentucky, parents ran a local general store, well thought of in the community. At 18 joined the army, smart and a good soldier rose through the ranks, Civil war started he aligned with the Union, through the war years ascended in rank to Brigadier General, retired in 1885, a widower, his wife, and two daughters died during a cholera epidemic, lives off the income from his family's stores, in 1884, hired Jacob Hacker as valet and companion, Hacker was his last aide de camp, very capable young man. General is well thought of, but recently over the past several years has been losing some of his mental capacity and has relied upon his valet for more.

Jacob Hacker, the valet of General, 27, born out west, parentage unknown, raised as an infant by numerous nannies hired by the General, entered the army, outstanding soldier excelling on the rifle range, later became General's valet and has been ever since. An unassuming young man with good manners and disappears into the background whenever appropriate and is always at hand to help the General through his memory lapses.

Mr. Professor Lucas Kane, 42, birthplace unknown probably near New York City, a practitioner of the occult, supernatural, lacks academic credentials, not a professor, opinions of him vary from great to charlatan, uses palm readings, seances, tells his subjects to meditate, laudanum while doing so. He preys on the gullible.

Captain Harvey Williams, 31, unmarried, little is known of his childhood, born out West, orphan, where the General was stationed, taken as a child by General, brought here with Jacob, lived in the household until he went out on his own, joined the police force, got rapidly routed up in the ranks, probably influenced by the General."

Washington took the liberty of ordering lunch for them, which

Holmes and Irene had neglected.

Holmes asks Washington, "Would Pinkerton be able to keep an unobserved watch over my suspects starting as soon as possible?"

"Yes, we could do that, but I would need the rest of the day to marshal forces for the task. How many agents will you need?"

"If, I let you know tomorrow morning, how soon can your people be ready for the task?"

"By early afternoon tomorrow."

Irene and Holmes bid Washington goodbye until tomorrow.

Scissor Grinding

May 16

7:00

P romptly at seven o'clock Holmes, in disguise, arrives at the scissor grinder's stable, reviews the sales prices, acquaints himself with the grinders stock of knives, scissors, repair parts, and other metal products. At eight o'clock he is on his way to the neighborhood.

Business is brisk, he has many customers requiring all manner of services from sharpening all types of cutting instruments to needing hardware for repairs.

While satisfying a customer, he sees a man approaching who had just left Mrs. Ambrose's residence.

He waits for his turn and says, "Where is Louis?"

"Louis asked me to do his neighborhood today since he won big at the races and had a wee bit too much of a good time."

"All right, sharpen these scissors and kitchen knives, and be quick about it."

While Holmes sharpens the instruments asks, "Are you the master of the house?"

"What concern of yours who I am? For your information, I am Mr. Eagers, butler to Mrs. Ambrose, mistress of the house, now get on with it."

After several minutes, Holmes finishes and gets a grudging nod of satisfaction from Eagers for the work, who pays and leaves.

Holmes thinks, no information there.

He just reaches the second house of his primary suspects, and there before him stands the housekeeper of the Colonel's house, Mrs. Lilith Matthews, she is a rather plain woman with a dour expression on her thin face.

Seeing Holmes, she asks, sourly "Where is Louis? Is he ill? I have relied upon him and his fine work for many years. Why do you have his wagon?"

"Ma'am, Louis did well at the races and had too much of good time to do his rounds today, and asked if I could do them."

"Well, I hope he gets well soon, but I do not know if I can rely upon you!"

"As for my work, I will do the very best I may, and if not acceptable, you will not have to pay."

"Alright", she says and hands him several scissors and knives.

She says, "If those knives are not sharpened properly, I will hear it from Mr. Matthews, my husband, he is quite particular as to the sharpness of the knives. He is a hunter and needs sharp knives to field dress the game he procures for the household."

"Aye", says Holmes, "He must be a grand shot to get so much game."

"Indeed he is, he has won many trophies for his skill with a rifle. Quite a sharpshooter. He learned when he was in the army with the Colonel."

"What kind of game does he hunt?"

"Anything edible from grouse to deer and they are all very delicious."

While sharpening, Holmes keeps talking endeavoring to learn as much as he can about the Colonel and Mr. Matthews, but Mrs. Matthews does not speak about the Colonel, except to say that the Colonel is a good man.

She irritatingly inquires, "Are you done?"

"Yes, Ma'am, I am. Please see if these are satisfactory."

She takes each item inspects them as says, "These will do."

Pays him accordingly, and heads back to the house.

Well, not much learned except Matthews is a sharpshooter and needs very sharp hunting knives. Holmes hopes that any encounter with the other households will supply more pertinent information.

Several more households need his services as he continues to work at his trade.

CHAPTER 45

Servant's Night Off

A t about ten-thirty, he is approached by a maid from Mr. Wilson's household with a few items to be sharpened.

She, Millie, is an impish girl of perhaps seventeen with red curly hair protruding under her maid's cap and a face filled with freckles. She shyly asks if he could help her.

Holmes says, "Aye, I can lass, and what do you have to be sharpened?"

"Just one knife for Mr. Henderson and a pair of scissors for the Housekeeper, Mrs. Watts."

"I'll do me best," he says and sets about doing it, asking her, "have you worked here very long?"

"No sir, just these past three months."

"Are you well treated?"

"Yes, sir, Mrs. Watts instructs me on how to do my job, and she does it nicely. Mr. Wilson is so kind and he does such wonderful works of charity for the truly poor, I could not ask for a better place to work, except sometimes Mr. Wilson seems sad because his rheumatism hurts him awful, and he is easily angered, but it don't last."

"That is too bad about Mr. Wilson, but it very well to hear that you are so well treated because some masters of the house are not so nice."

"He is nice, and the other masters are also very good. The staffs of some of the houses are being given Thursday night and Friday off and there is a big paid appreciation party for all of us at a hotel in town."

"That sounds grand, which houses are doing this?"

"Mine, the General's, Mrs. Ambrose's and the Colonel's'"

"Well, I hope you have a marvelous time."

"I am sure we will."

He finishes and she is off with the sharpened items.

"Thank you and goodbye."

Holmes thinks the servants are to be gone on Thursday the eighteenth and Friday the nineteenth, the perfect time for the killing.

CHAPTER 46

The Last House

A nother hour passes, and the business begins to lessen, and his vocal cords are tiring from constantly shouting "Scissors and knives"

12:00
He is fast approaching the last residence and no one is in sight to get his services, he passes the house slowing his pace slightly, and looks longingly for a hint of interest, but none appears.

He begins to hasten, when he hears a slurred, "Hey, grinder, I need some work done."

Turning Holmes sees a man ambling toward him, he is below average height, slightly bulky, which appears to be from muscle and not fat.

Holmes pulls up and says, "Lucky I heard you sir, and what might I do for you?"

"You are early today and the maid forgot to bring these knives to you."

Holmes notices that the knives are not for kitchen work or cleaning game, but almost surgical in their appearance.

"Aye, it's not been a busy day. Let's see what ye have."

Excitedly, he says, "You are not Louis, where is he?"

"Louis won big at the races and the winnings went to his head if you get my drift, so I've taken his route for the day."

"He does a great job on my knives, I need them razor sharp. I hope you are nearly as good?"

"As far as how good I am, you'll need to tell me but if not satisfactory, you'll not have to pay me. Are you the master of the house, sir?"

"Of course not, this is General Wellington's home and I am his valet, Mr. Hacker, now get on with it."

Holmes notices that while speaking Hacker's eyes dart all about hardly focusing on the grinder. He has pointed teeth and his physical appearance is of one born of a mother who suffered from disease and passing it on to her child at birth. In all likelihood, the father of the child also had the disease and passed it on or may have gotten it from the woman.

"Well, sir, I am done, and I think you could shave with these."

Hacker carefully examines the blades and pays the full price with a generous tip. Smiling with his pointed teeth, he departs saying "Louis had better not take many days off or he will lose his customers, this is first-grade work, Good day." With that said trundles off.

"Thank you, sir and I am as pleased that you are."

Once he is alone, Holmes remarks to himself, "What an unusual man and he appears overly pleased with the sharpness of his knives."

There is no more business so he starts the journey back to the stable with a lot to think about.

Arriving at the stable he is met by Louis, who inquires what kind of day he had.

Holmes responds, "Very encouraging, and I met many interesting parties who wondered where you were, I gave them the racing story and they accepted it. Here are the receipts and a very nice tip from the General's valet."

"Well done and that valet, Jacob, is a weird one. He is never satisfied with my work and he cherishes his knives as if they were his children. He gives me the chills if you know what I mean."

"I do, yes the chills. His eyes are always darting here and there and never maintaining his gaze upon whomever he is speaking to. Well, now I must be on my way, is it possible to catch a cab here."

"Yes sir, they come by quite frequently. I will see if I can get one for you."

"Thank you."

Several minutes later, Louis has a cab waiting for Holmes, and upon entering, he says to Louis, "Keep this little adventure between us."

"That I will and thank you for a day off and your generosity, and now I feel like I truly won at the races. Good day."

1:00
In the cab, Holmes is on his way to the hotel, removes his disguise, and the driver takes no notice of the change in his appearance. Holmes pays the cabbie and enters the hotel.

CHAPTER 47

A Visitor

1:30

Entering the hotel room, Sherlock senses the smell of tobacco in the air. Irene greets him very warmly, and he says, "I assume we had a guest while I was out, and I believe it was Captain Williams. If I am not mistaken."

"Yes, we did, or I did. And it was the Captain who arrived unannounced and was asking for you and wondered where you were, I told him sometimes you need solitude to clear your brain, and you do not even let me know where you are going. Eventually, you will return and are usually chipper, and ready to have dinner. I pray that I did not say anything amiss."

"No, my dear, you did not, and I am in a much better mood."

Sherlock peers at the ashtray, he gathers the ash in his hands, examines it, he knows at once what it is.

He moves to the gramophone and places on it a rather loud and long recording, and taking Irene by the hand, he leans in and whispers, " I shall search the rooms looking for another listening device."

For the next half an hour, Irene and Sherlock exchange pleasantries on a myriad of topics while he silently tears the rooms apart searching for any sign of another listening device, and puts it together again. He finds nothing and is certain that the rooms are not subject to outside listening.

The music plays until Sherlock turns it off, and says to Irene, "The room is not subjected to outside listening. So we may once again be ourselves and I will tell you all about this morning's work."

"But first, I am certain that someone is trying to follow me, but I slipped by him. But we must be alert at all times, I, we, are now apparently making the culprits extremely nervous."

Irene laughingly says, "You seem to be extremely good at making people nervous."

"This tobacco ash I found here is the same as the ones I gathered at the other crime sites, and it is apparent the Captain has not been completely honest about the ash."

He told her about the scissor grinding business saying, "I became quite adept at the task, found out that Matthews is a sharpshooter, Hacker likes his unusual knives razor-sharp, Wilson has bouts with anger, brought on by attacks of rheumatism, or so I was told by a young maid and finally and most important the staffs of these houses have Thursday night and Friday off for a party given by their employers."

Irene responds, "It would seem Thursday would be a good evening for the final murder."

"My thought exactly."

2:30
He says, "I need to call Washington and the Colonel."

Irene responds, "Well, let us be about it. You need your sentry."

"Yes, I do."

CHAPTER 48

Help Needed

They leave the hotel and head to the telephone exchange directly, now is not the time to waste time trying to evade followers. They are both armed.

At the telephone exchange, Irene stands guard and Holmes calls Washington.

He answers, Holmes identifies himself and says, "I believe that the act will take place on Thursday night or early Friday morning. Are you able to arrange for as many as eight agents to be here this evening?"

"That is a tall order but I believe so."

"Call the hotel and if I am not in leave a message for me which will just be a name, Watson, and I will call you as soon as I can. If I answer just say, Watson."

"Agreed, goodbye."

3:00
Holmes places another call, this one to Colonel Waterson.

His call is directed to the Colonel and Holmes starts without the usual hellos.

"Colonel, are there any other police in the vicinity of Louisville?"

"Well hello to you Mr. Wallace, and yes there is a county sheriff who has police responsibilities over the county."

"Do you know him?"

"I know the man, Sheriff Patrick O'Malley because occasionally some of my soldiers have gotten into trouble in Louisville and the local police did nothing about it since it was only a bar fight in the red light district and the only ones hurt were prostitutes, but the sheriff arrested my men, notified the fort and awaited my sergeant and a squad of men to come and get them."

"I am so sorry to bother you, again, but it is urgent I have your opinion about Sheriff O'Malley."

"The sheriff has expressed no love for the Captain. I have a most favorable opinion of the sheriff and believe whatever he is told remains with him, and I have the impression the sheriff would like nothing better than having a good run at the Louisville police, especially the Captain. The sheriff is a true police officer."

"That is exactly what I needed to hear because I cannot rely on the Louisville police, and I need a good law enforcement officer to help me. Once again, I apologize for bothering you, but would you please contact the sheriff right now and tell him I need his help desperately and confirm to him my credentials?"

"Now I am a messenger, alright Mr. Wallace, I will do that immediately. If I do or do not contact him, where will I call you?"

Holmes gives him the exchange telephone number, and asks, "Do you have the sheriff's office telephone number." The Colonel gives him the sheriff's number.

3:30
The Colonel calls back and says, "The sheriff will let you call him. Well, good luck, and if I may be of help please contact me."

"Thank you very much and your help may end this ordeal."

CHAPTER 49

O'Malley

H olmes contacts Sheriff O'Malley and after a gruff answer by the sheriff.

Holmes says, "You no doubt are aware of the rash of murders in Louisville with no arrests. I became involved early on when my wife and I discovered Mr, Vincent's corpse at Churchill Downs, and all of these deaths are connected to a devilish cult. I would like to meet with you as soon as possible, and by no means let the Louisville police know of our meeting."

The sheriff listens attentively and says, "Yes, I am well aware of the killings and the lack of progress on their solution. If you can shed some light on the matter, I would very much like to meet with you, and the way you have expressed it, you do not want the Louisville police to know that we are meeting."

"Yes, I do not believe they are eager to bring these killers to justice."

The sheriff says, "I will meet you in my office, as soon as you can get here. Goodbye."

"I will be right there and thank you."

CHAPTER 50

Sheriff O'Malley

4:00

S herlock and Irene leave the telephone exchange and hire a carriage taking a leisurely drive around the city to assess whether they are being followed, once he is certain they are safe, they are driven to the Sheriff's headquarters

4:30

They arrive and they are whisked into the Sheriff's office, which is secluded from the other offices by a meeting room, not in use, and a room for interrogations also unoccupied, this minimizes the chance of being overheard.

Sheriff Patrick O'Malley is a sturdy man of about fifty years, nearly six feet tall possessing a deep bass voice, long sideburns a bushy mustache, and the complexion of a man liking his drink.

He begins, "Mr. Wallace, if that is your name, I will listen to what you have to say since Colonel Waterson says you are a lawman of grand accomplishments."

"I appreciate the Colonel's confidence in me. He has been told by Captain Williams who has been in touch with the English authorities who have attested to my character and expertise in criminal matters."

"I accept the Colonel's affirmation of your credentials. I know of the murders, but they, the Louisville police, never work too hard when it is only a prostitute that is beaten or killed. Only one was killed in Louisville, the other across the Ohio in Indiana. Surely, they must have some suspects for the killings of the others. If not, they are truly not doing the job"

"Well, neither woman was killed where they were found since there was scant blood found at those scenes. I believe they were killed elsewhere, bled out at elsewhere but both were killed on this side of the river."

"Could be, but what does it have to do with me?"

"Please bear with me as I present you with some history of the murders of numerous prostitutes, all slain in the same manner. Five years ago in France, three were killed by having their throats cut, three killed in Italy with severed throats, four butchered the same way in London by Jack the Ripper, five murdered in a similar fashion in the Northeastern United States, New York, and Massachusetts, and now two have been subjected to the same hideous death here in the Louisville environs. Seventeen prostitutes killed in the same brutal fashion with scant blood found where they were discarded in death. I am certain an eighteenth will soon join the others and will be slain and drained of her blood in the next two days. All of these women, I believe, were murdered by the same man or men, and I know the Captain has been covering up for the culprits and maybe one himself."

"Outrageous", bellows the Sheriff, " I do not care one cent for the Captain, but a murderer or an accomplice, he cannot be."

Holmes, "Let me share with you, a letter written by Mr. Vincent, that I found in a safe in his hiding place in the Louisville Public Warehouse."

Holmes hands the letter to the Sheriff, and O'Malley reads it.

Handing the letter back to Holmes, he says, "I find this hard to believe, but the corruption of the Captain, I do believe."

"Vincent was killed because he tried to blackmail individuals associated with the cult. Maybe he tried Mrs. Ambrose, the paramour, or Lucas Kane, spiritualist. The other five murdered begins with the killing of the two thugs who transported Vincent's body to the race track, Nichols' assassination, the person who listened in on conversations in my hotel suite, and the informant of Nichols' location. All five of these have to do with the investigation of Vincent's death. All in all, eight killed including the two murdered prostitutes, and no suspects identified by the police."

He continues, "Now I will proceed to lay out the chronology of the crimes. First, the murder of Vincent, the Captain upon arrival at the stable where Vincent was found was going to write the death off as a heart attack, but I presented him with my findings, and he reluctantly agreed Vincent was probably murdered and the two men who transported Vincent to the stable, were executed the next day by their employer because they knew too much."

Continuing Holmes says, "The Captain indicated that Vincent was probably blackmailing someone and they had done him in. My wife and I went to the Derby Gala and came up with a list of potential persons, who might be potentially blackmailed by Vincent. Blackmail being something Vincent had been suspected of doing to keep himself in the posh life he led."

The Sheriff says, "I had heard about Vincent and thought he might have been done in by someone he was blackmailing."

Holmes continues, "As I said, my wife and I casually met and conversed with all of those on our list at the Derby Gala."

Nichols Disclosure

"One conversation, in particular, was significant. Mr. Nichols, who was inebriated, was upset when another of this group dismissed the dead prostitute as nothing to be concerned about. He said she, Evelyn, was just a young lost soul. After a little more conversation the little group broke up."

"The next day, I mentioned the prostitute's name to the Captain, he was surprised I knew it, and he wanted to know where I learned the name and told him, Nichols. He set out looking for Nichols to see what he knew. Nichols knew who Evelyn had as a customer and had told him. He hid out trying to escape, was caught and conveniently assassinated while in the hands of the Captain's men and as I was holding Nichols ever so lightly a second shot was fired, and as I stumbled the bullet went through my hat and struck Nichols. The second bullet, I am certain was meant for me, but my stumbling saved my life."

"After my luckily escaping a fatal shot to my head, my wife and I received this anonymous note threatening us and confirming the intent to murder me at the Nichols' scene."

Holmes hands the note to the Sheriff, who reads it and hands it back.

"I requested information via telegraph to find if the people on my list were in the vicinity of numerous similar killings in England and on the continent, seven of the list were at all the sights. My first telegram was not answered, or if it was I never got the reply. I went to Fort Knox and re-sent the telegram, and received a reply stating they had previously sent the information."

"Some of the people on my list were in the vicinity of the

crimes, numerous times, including the Captain and a Mr. Kane. I wondered how the Captain could travel to all these places on his wages."

"Another incriminating factor was tobacco ash found at the scene of the Vincent murder, I traced to a unique blend ordered by several of the listed people. This same ash was found at the execution of the thugs, in the rooms of the sniper who killed Nichols, only one sniper, the other spot was a decoy making me believe that there were two, since the Captain, the shooter's accomplice, knew which exit from the brothel would be used, so only one shooter was needed to make the shot. The ash was left I surmise because the Captain and his accomplices were baiting me. The Captain also had the cigars that made the damning ash, but he said it was a gift, but one of the dead thugs had a cigar of that kind in his possession, and there was ash on the river stones. Almost as soon as I was on the case, the telephone in my suite at the hotel had a listening device attached so any conversation in the suite would be overheard by another. The listener was later discovered dead at his listening post."

"Lastly, the Captain is an integral part of this case. First, he was going to say Vincent succumbed to a heart attack. Next, the two thugs involved with Vincent were identified and very quickly killed. The telephone listening device was found and the listener was murdered. Nichols was found and assassinated. The Nichols informant had his throat cut very soon after Nichols was killed. None of these persons' names were public information, but information the Captain had, and I am convinced he passed it on to others in the cult to clean up any potential leaks to the police."

Concluding he said, "Well, there you have it, let me have your opinion."

The Sheriff says, "You lay out a good case, but it is only circumstantial. You have no real proof."

"That is true, but I have a plan to get hard evidence.""

"And that is?", asks the Sheriff.

"We have to catch them in the act."

CHAPTER 52

The Plan

5:30 PM

"And how do you propose to do that?"

"I have hired Pinkerton of Cincinnati to follow my ten suspects. I believe the deed is planned for this Thursday. Two days from now, since that is when the servants have a special night off and all day off on Friday."

"Why Pinkerton, and not my men?"

"I thought, your men might be known to the suspects."

"It is unlikely they know my men, very seldom do we patrol the city, and when people see a copper they only see the uniform.

"You offer may make Pinkerton unnecessary, and I will need at least ten men to watch the suspects."

"Ten is a big number, I can only spare four, but they will be the best and most loyal to me, and should be invisible when not in uniform."

"That is good, I will arrange for the rest from Pinkerton."

"Where might the deed be done?"

CHAPTER 53

Suspects Revealed

H olmes sighs and says, "In the basement of the General's house."

"What, that cannot be, he is an outstanding member of our community."

"Yes, he is and he is losing his senses and is in the latter stages of syphilis."

"That's absurd man!"

"Not truly, how long have you known him? Has he changed in that time, physically or mentally?"

"Physically, he is the same only older."

"Has he always worn a wig and gloves at all times?"

"No, just in the past few years." he pauses, "Are you saying these are signs of the disease."

"Yes, in later stages, patches of hair fall out and the hands are gnarled and swollen, blistered and red all the time. Hence the gloves and the wig."

"All right, what else?"

"In conversation, he seems to wander off, and then repeat himself. This is another sign, a loss of mental faculties. Have you noticed it?"

"Yes, but many older people have such a problem. In your scheme, who are the others besides the General?"

"The General's ward, or should I say son, Jacob Hacker, who bears an uncanny resemblance to the General. The young man bears the signs of the disease having been passed onto a newborn by his mother, who was a carrier. He has pointed teeth like a screwdriver, and he has a love for his razor-sharp knives which I sharpened for him."

"The child's mother had the disease, possibly given to her by the General. My supposition is that the General caught the disease when he was on military duty out west."

"Next would be the Captain."

"Why the Captain?

"His motives could be manifold, assurance of wealth after the General dies, or he could be a relation."

"Good God, the Captain was brought here with Jacob, lived in the household until he went out on his own, joined the police force, and quickly advanced to Captain. I am certain the General was a great aid to him."

"Next is Mrs. Ambrose and her butler, William Eagers; Colonel Hawthorne; Charles Wilson and his valet, Samuel Henderson, and finally, Lucas Kane, the occultist, and confidant of Mrs. Ambrose."

"Now do you see?"

"Yes, but it is still circumstantial."

"Indeed, that is why we must catch them in the act!"

The Capture Plan

"What is your plan?"

"We are handicapped, because we cannot rely on the Louisville police, and must have our own way to circumvent that weakness is by having you make the necessary arrests. Our manpower will be the use of Pinkertons and your deputies. We have nine suspects, six suspects residing two each in three separate houses, two live alone, and the last is the Colonel."

Holmes lays out the plan as follows, "We need two shifts of seven watchers with one being the lead, and the six others will be working in two twelve-hour shifts switching off between suspects to not be spotted with each having a cab waiting, and when needed following a suspect, the cabs are also on a twelve-hour shift and each cab will have a bicycle in order to have the agent watch the suspect and the driver to use the bicycle to go to the nearest telephone exchange office and send the alert to you, Sheriff. You will when notified call me at the hotel and say "the game is afoot." I will then move to the General's house using the cab, I will have waiting outside the hotel."

"It is quite a plan and feasible. I would like to add two more deputies to your list. One to keep watch over your wife and another stationed in your hotel's lobby for security."

Holmes says, "Yes, and I appreciate the concern. Please make your arrangements with Mr. Washington of Pinkerton."

Sheriff O'Malley calls Mr. Washington and they map out the coverage of deputies and Pinkerton agents on the suspects, and set the plan in motion, immediately.

CHAPTER 55

Waiting and Watching

May 17 Wednesday

E arly on the morning of Wednesday, the seventeenth, the deputies and Pinkertons are all in place, the second shift men are clandestinely housed in a vacant house near the General's home. They are eagerly awaiting the signal.

Holmes to keep up the subterfuge calls the Captain asking, "What news do you have?"

"We are hunting a suspect. He is a mentally ill person with numerous attacks on people using knives. We should have him soon, and you will be able to question him when he is custody."

"That is good news indeed, I look forward to the opportunity to question him. Goodbye."

The rest of the day passes without any unusual movement, except Hacker goes to the brothel and after a short stay heads back to the General's house.

Holmes waits anxiously for the signal and has a carriage ready both day and night, but nothing happens on Wednesday.

CHAPTER 56

Movement and Abduction

May 18 Thursday

10: AM

On Thursday, Holmes once again seeks an update and gets the same reply from the Captain.

Nearly two days have passed, the General has not left his house, Jacob is constantly on the move in the General's carriage, and frequents the brothels, but leaves returning home each day.

9:00 PM

After dark on Thursday, Jacob heads back to the brothel, where Nichols was shot, picks up the Captain in a darkened alley. They ride together to the back of the brothel, but the Captain remains secreted in the carriage, while Jacob enters the rear entrance and immediately exits with a young woman, who leaves voluntarily with him. Once in the carriage, they depart.

The deputy sends the message to the Sheriff. The Sheriff receives the message and calls Holmes with "the games is afoot" message. Holmes rushes out to his waiting cab.

As he approaches the cab, he feels the barrel of a pistol pressed into his back, and Lucas Kane says, "Off for a carriage ride Mr. Wallace, or should I say Mr. Sherlock Holmes? I would like very much to shoot you right here, but the noise may bother the fine people on the street. So please enter the cab quickly and join Colonel Hawthorne." Once inside, the cab starts.

As planned, the sheriff has assigned deputies to watch Wallace and Irene. The deputy assigned this task sees the abduction but is too far away to intervene, instead, he hurries into the hotel and commandeers a telephone, and calls the sheriff.

The sheriff is almost out the door when he hears the telephone and haltingly returns to answer, the deputy says, "They have abducted Mr. Wallace and I will follow."

"Stay close, but if it looks like they are not going to the General's house intercept them and save Mr. Wallace, but if they are on their way to the house stay back, but be ready to assault the house when we arrive."

"Yes sir."

Plan in Motion

T he sheriff heads to the rendezvous location to meet the rest of his men all of whom are praying they are not too late.

The Sheriff has a drawing of the interior of the house from the city building department. With this information they know where the cellar entrance is located and how it is best to enter the house without making their presence known.

The carriage with Holmes, Kane, and the Colonel arrives at the General's house.

Holmes says, "Well, I was right, the General is in the midst of this gruesome enterprise."

Kane shoves Holmes and says, "A lot of good that will do you. Be a nice English gentleman and move to that door, and you will have all of your questions answered. Now move!"

Holmes, Kane, and the Colonel enter through an unlocked door. Once inside they are on a stairway landing, they move down the steps and enter through another door into a large lighted basement which houses a modest wine cellar, coal bins, and assorted barrels.

The door is closed. Kane prods Holmes with the revolver towards the wine racks, the Colonel pulls on the middle shelf, the rack moves inward and discloses an opening into another room. While this goes on, Holmes has been unobtrusively dropping cigar ash on the floor, he stumbles and puts an open packet of ash on the middle shelf while coughing, hoping that it leads the sheriff to the hidden room.

CHAPTER 58

The Killing Room

The wine cellar shelf is pulled shut and Holmes and his abductors are greeted by the room's occupants, General Wellington, Jacob Hacker, Charles Wilson, Samuel Henderson, Mrs. Gloria Ambrose, William Eagers, and Captain Williams.

They almost in unison say, "Welcome, Mr. Holmes."

Hacker laughs saying, "I knew who you were once I saw you when your Scotland Yard coppers were looking for me, Jack the Ripper. You didn't stop me then and you won't now, will ya?"

Ignoring Hacker, Holmes immediately sees a young woman suspended from the ceiling with her legs and arms spreadeagled, she is facing down, seemingly unconscious, and probably heavily drugged. Below her head is a large silver tub and he knows it is there to catch her blood once they cut her throat.

Holmes shouts, "The nine of you are all beyond insanity, you make evil look like child's play."

With that Holmes is struck in the back of the head by Kane who says, "Be well-mannered non-believer and have a seat to view the ceremony, it will be the last thing you see and your beautiful wife will never know what became of you, and I will be there to console her."

The Colonel leaves Kane guarding Holmes and puts on a red robe like the others in the room who are also wearing crimson robes and hoods with gold bunting festooned with a black pentagram in a circle and each holds a knife, some of which Holmes may have sharpened.

Kane does not leave his post but puts his pistol away while putting on his robe, Holmes takes the moment, leaves the chair, grasps Kane by the robe, and flings him towards the others. Kane has lost the gun, the others rise and begin to rush Holmes, just as the wine shelf door is ripped open and Sheriff O'Malley, his four deputies, Washington, and his four Pinkertons flood the room.

Henderson throws his knife at the advancing deputies striking one but another deputy fires his revolver striking him in the shoulder bringing him down. The wounded officer although injured holds Henderson down until others can relieve him.

The other officers and Pinkertons seize the remaining robed occupants, but Hacker flies from his seat, evades capture, and with his blade raised rushes to the poor girl hung from the ceiling, but just before he reaches her, Holmes tackles him, and the two grapple on the floor. Hacker swears venomously and tries to slash Holmes, his knife making a slight cut in Holmes' shoulder, but Holmes subdues him.

The young unconscious woman is lowered from the ceiling, untied, and carried out of the basement. The Sheriff, his deputies, and the Pinkertons take control of the other eight, shackle them, with their hands in front of them, and make them sit on the floor of the killing room.

The General, who is cursing and threatening everyone is frothing at the mouth and is evidently quite insane.

There was the subdued Hacker with a look of unrequited blood lust in his eyes.

Wilson is shaking uncontrollably saying, "Now my pain will never go away."

His valet, Henderson, screams, "All the harlots must die!"

The Colonel is livid demanding he be set free.

Captain Williams sits quite still but begins to sob.

Lucas Kane is serene and silent.

Mrs. Ambrose being held down by her butler, Eagers, screeches, "You do not know what you have done, we are trying to save the world and you have released the hounds of hell. She was to die at midnight on the eighteenth."

Then she starts to wail.

At that point, the General shouts "It is undone Lucifer, we failed and now we must see you in person. Have mercy on our souls!"

The eight raise their hands, open the lid on a Borgia ring they each wear swallow the contents, and within minutes they are all dead.

Hacker tries to get free, but is stopped by Holmes and a deputy, he is shackled with his hands behind him. His ring is removed from his finger, and Holmes opens the lid sees the contents, smells it, and by its odor it is cyanide, a quick deadly poison. Hacker begins gibbering like a madman and has a seizure falling to the floor, but not likely to die from it.

The Sheriff says, "This is a fine mess. We capture all of them, we think, and they kill themselves, all but this lunatic. How do we explain their deaths?"

"There is only one left, so we charge him with all the murders including these eight, whom he poisoned. No need to sensationalize this, no one will be served any good by telling this tale. We have the slasher and must bring him to trial for the murders."

Holmes, "Today is the eighteenth, and tonight the eighteenth victim was to be murdered."

Subterranean Storage Room

10:00 PM

H olmes walks away from the others and searches the killing room, and in a corner of the room under a rug finds a trap door, and upon opening sees a staircase leading to a subterranean room which is much colder, with a cold stream running through it.

On the floor are seventeen clear jugs containing what appears to be blood. Each jug is labeled with the names and dates of the seventeen murdered women killed by Hacker and his accomplices.

He finds a journal with the cult's doctrine, elaborately written. In summary, they believed by murdering these women, drinking their co-mingled blood, they would, as Vincent laid out, attain wealth, long life, good health, be cured of any affliction, and be raised on the throne of Lucifer, the great anti-god architect of the universe.

The journal lists the names of those captured and the late Mr. Nichols as members of this cult, hence his statement that the ten are now nine. The cult was started by Lucas Kane, who through the use of drugs manipulated the members and warped their minds with his pronouncements as the word of the anti-god.

Returning to the killing room, Holmes calls the Sheriff over, shows him the journal, and relates to him the seventeen jugs of blood in the lower basement, all cataloged by name of murdered women.

CHAPTER 60

The Story

I t was decided to remove the robes from the dead cult members, carry their corpses to the main living room, and arrange them as if they were having a sociable evening until they were poisoned by Hacker.

Those who viewed the scene include senior constables of Sheriff O'Malley's department and Washington's Pinkertons, all are instructed to keep what went on here a secret, never to be spoken about even with each other. The case was a horrible poisoning by a madman, who was captured and who will be remanded to the Sheriff's jail.

The unconscious drugged prostitute is taken back to her brothel and the madam is told that she was found on the street.

The jugs of blood are opened and the contents poured into the stream flowing through the lower basement, the labels are removed from the jugs and the jugs smashed.

The robes of the cult members, their knives, and other paraphernalia of the cult are gathered up.

The robes are burned in the furnace along with the journal, jug tags, and Borgia rings.

The basement and sub-basement are examined one last time before being sealed by the deputies.

Holmes says, "Thus ends the string of murders over two continents with twenty-three dead, plus the eight suicides, tonight. Thirty-one dead for the cult. Truly insane."

The sheriff agrees.

The Sheriff summons the department's photographer to come

to the General's house and take photos of the dead in the living room to substantiate the poisoning tale.

The dead are removed to the county morgue for autopsies which would reveal that they were indeed poisoned. The one gunshot is attributed to Hacker as he forced Henderson to take the poison.

The sheriff says to Holmes, "I will station an officer at each of the descendants' households and inform the servants what transpired while they were gone. They will be told to keep on with their duties for the time being.

CHAPTER 61

Return to Irene

May 19 Friday

2:00 AM

S herlock enters the hotel suite, and immediately Irene is in his arms hugging him tightly and says, "I am so happy to see you my love." and kisses him passionately.

"And I to see you my dear, it has been a harrowing night, let me sit and I will tell you all about it."

He starts with his hotel abduction, the Sheriff's rescue of him and the young prostitute, the suicides of the cult members, the incarceration of Jacob Hacker, actually Jack the Ripper, the covering up of the cult's actions, and the placement of blame on Hacker.

Incredulously she says, "Why, not the truth?"

"Sometimes the truth will hurt many more people, and to what end. All, but one, of them, is dead, and he is insane and will spend the rest of his days in an asylum, or be hanged for his crimes."

"But the others will be thought of as victims, not murderers."

"True, but they are victims of Lucas Kane who drugged them into this grotesque fantasy of curing illness, finding solace, gaining power, gaining wealth, being made to look like others, and the list goes on. You said Kane preys on the lost and alone, he was a cruel leader of the cult and he also paid the price."

"I understand, but won't it all come out?"

"I do not think it can be proved, the garments, the book, the blood, the knives, the hidden killing room, the rings and all the rest have been destroyed. The most trusted deputies of the Sheriff and Pinkerton have been sworn to secrecy and being God-fearing men, they truly believe they have done God's will by keeping silent for benefit of the people of Louisville. The young prostitute was drugged by the cult and did not remember anything of the killing room, or what took place after she rode away in the carriage, and even her memory of that is foggy.

"Right now, my love, I am foggy and I need sleep."

"Yes, dear."

And off to bed, they go.

CHAPTER 62

A New Day

May 19 Friday

8 AM

I rene is awakened by the telephone ringing in the suite, Sherlock stirs but does not wake. She rushes to answer the telephone.

"Hello"

The Sheriff replies, "Mrs. Wallace may I speak to your husband."

"He still sleeps."

Sherlock enters the room saying, "I am awake dear, who is it on the telephone?"

"It is the Sheriff."

She hands him the phone, "Good morning O'Malley, what has happened?"

There is a pause, and the Sheriff says, "It is not a good morning, Jacob Hacker has killed himself."

"What!"

"When we got him to the station, he was searched and everything was taken from him. We did not expect suicide, but he did it."

"How?"

"He had a small razor-sharp knife in the sole of his shoe. When the guards were bringing him breakfast, he showed the knife and yelled, "I am coming to you father!" and he cut his throat and died within minutes. There was nothing my men could do to save him."

"I understand, now there will be no trial, just a burial."

"The case ends with another death. What a waste of life."

"True, the city will be in shock, but it will not be prolonged by a trial and potential execution. The city will return to normal. I thank you Sheriff O'Malley for all you and your select deputies have done to bring to a close this horrific enterprise of devil worship."

"Between us, I thank you for having trusted me, Mr. Wallace or should I say Mr. Sherlock Holmes. I am an avid reader of Dr. Watson's stories of your exploits, I was suspicious before you brought up the tobacco ash, and then I was convinced, Mr. Holmes. Your secret is secure with me and I will tell no one."

"I am thankful for your discretion, and someday you will know why it must be so. Thank you, again and goodbye."

Hanging the telephone up, he turns to Irene and says, "Jacob Hacker, Jack the Ripper, has cut his own throat and died."

"How ghastly! He must truly have been insane."

"Yes, he and they were. And Sheriff O'Malley knows who I am, he has read all of Watson's stories, but he vows to keep it secret"

"He is quite the gentleman, now let us have breakfast, put this behind us, but before we do, my love, I must say, you did solve this case, Mr. Sherlock Holmes"

Just then, there is a knock at the door. Holmes answers the door and finds a page with a telegram addressed to Irene. He tips the lad and takes the telegram to her. She opens it and reads aloud, "Is it possible for Bohemian Escape to race in the fifth race today since we had a late scratch. Please give me a call at the track office before ten. Thank you."

Irene says, "What do you think?"

"I think we should get ready to go to the races but first have someone check all of the adjacent stalls for any bodies."

"Yes, I will do it right now, especially the bodies' part."

And they both laugh.

Made in the USA
Monee, IL
03 August 2021